T0198633

The *Gleeful* Banker

RICHARD FAIRSING

BALBOA.
PRESS
A DIVISION OF HAY HOUSE

Balboa Press books may be ordered through booksellers or by contacting:

Balboa Press
A Division of Hay House
1663 Liberty Drive
Bloomington, IN 47403
www.balboapress.com
1 (877) 407-4847

Because of the dynamic nature of the Internet, any web addresses or
links contained in this book may have changed since publication and
may no longer be valid. The views expressed in this work are solely those
of the author and do not necessarily reflect the views of the publisher,
and the publisher hereby disclaims any responsibility for them.

The author of this book does not dispense medical advice or prescribe the use
of any technique as a form of treatment for physical, emotional, or medical
problems without the advice of a physician, either directly or indirectly. The
intent of the author is only to offer information of a general nature to help
you in your quest for emotional and spiritual well-being. In the event you use
any of the information in this book for yourself, which is your constitutional
right, the author and the publisher assume no responsibility for your actions.

Any people depicted in stock imagery provided by Thinkstock are models,
and such images are being used for illustrative purposes only.
Certain stock imagery © Thinkstock.

Print information available on the last page.

ISBN: 978-1-5043-3454-9 (sc)
ISBN: 978-1-5043-3456-3 (hc)
ISBN: 978-1-5043-3455-6 (e)

Library of Congress Control Number: 2015909268

Balboa Press rev. date: 06/16/2015

CHAPTER ONE

Suddenly awake, Samantha squinted at the glowing red numbers on the alarm clock. They read five a.m. In fifteen minutes it would begin to blare. Fully awake, she reached over and shut off its pending alert.

"God, I don't feel like running this morning. It's such a hassle trying to maintain my figure. I'm nearly fifty years old and I'm trying to look like I'm thirty. I don't know how long I can keep it up. Hell, most women my age can't fit their derrieres into a large gunny sack. But what's the point? All Dave wants from a wife is a quick lay every week or so and lots of food and beer every night. He must be 50 pounds overweight. I can't understand his attitude. His father died, from a coronary, when he was fifty. Dave's almost fifty one and he sounds like a bull moose when he climbs a flight of stairs. Nobody, including Dave, knows what the hell his blood pressure is...probably best not to know. He wouldn't do anything about it if it were off the chart. He could go anytime and if he does, I'll be back on the auction block. If I'm going to bring any kind of a price, I'll have to look the part. I suppose that's why I expend all my energy trying to keep the old chassis looking good.

Dave might be a slob but he's a successful one. He's like most bankers, he makes a lot of money. It's certainly enough to allow us to live comfortably in this snobby neighborhood. I suspect, though, it's money not well spent." She concluded.

1

She was about to get out of bed when her husband turned over and slung an arm over her waist. Fearful that he might be interested in a morning session, she slipped out from under his arm. As she did, she remembered she had to wake him. He had to be at the local airport in a little more than an hour.

"Dave!" She shouted. "Up, up now, your plane leaves in a couple of hours and you have to be on it. Do you hear me? Up." she repeated.

"God damn it Samantha! Stop screaming like a goddamn banshee. I know, I know." He said as he rolled out from the far side of the bed.

"Fine! Fine, Dave! Just another example of the thanks I get from you. If it weren't for me, you wouldn't get your lazy ass out of bed for your own funeral."

Thinking about what she had just said, Samantha wondered what had prompted her to use such a strange expression.

I was probably hoping, subconsciously, for his demise." She thought, while mildly chastising herself for thinking such.

"Aren't you cute this morning?" Dave countered. "If I miss the plane, can I use one of your broomsticks to fly to New York?"

"You could, Dave, if you lost 50 pounds."

"You know, Samantha, I'm really looking forward to this trip. Do you know why?"

"I can guess, Dave. I can guess" she replied as she left the room.

After completing her morning's routine in the bathroom, she emerged wearing her jogging outfit and went into the kitchen to begin preparing breakfast. Normally, she jogged on an empty stomach. But this morning she thought she would share a light breakfast with Dave. She had just finished preparing it, when her husband, dressed in a business suit, entered the kitchen.

"I appreciate you making chow Sam. The only thing you get on a flight nowadays is a scented picture of a bag of peanuts." he grumbled as he sat down at the breakfast table.

"Well, make sure you go before you get on board. I hear they're charging twenty dollars to use the john."

Dave briefly acknowledged his wife's quip. But then, he quickly returned his attention to the white of his wife's hips that showed thru the slits in her black shorts as she dashed from one kitchen chore to another. His interest in her appearance intensified when she bent over to load the dish washer. Her long black hair tumbled over her shoulders to partially hide her white breasts' struggle to ascend the sagging neckline of her black jersey.

"God, she's still a beautiful women." he murmured as he looked down at his groin and continued as though he were speaking to someone; "Down, down, you growing beast, your master has other plans for you."

"I'm sorry Dave, what did you say?"

"Oh, oh nothing really, Sam, I was just thinking out loud. If you're anxious to go off on your romp in the woods, go ahead. I'll clean up here before I leave. You are still running, through the woods, aren't you?"

"Yes, I love the feeling of being close to nature, when I run there. But I'm in no rush. I'll wait until you've finished." As she sat down at the table, she thought; "That's strange. He usually warns me about running in the woods. Oh well, Dave is Dave and he can be strange indeed, at times."

Dave lifted his cup, to his lips, and drained its contents. He stood up and then bent over to peck Samantha on the check.

"I'll call you late tonight when I get to London. If it gets too late, I'll call you tomorrow. I've got to run. Hope you enjoy your run, I'm gone." Dave said while closing the front door behind him.

Samantha finished cleaning up the kitchen and then left the house, pausing only to lock the front door.

Sometimes, she ran around the artificial lake that centered their upscale village. But this morning she decided she would run in the wooded area that separated the wealthy from the rest of the city's population. Dave had cautioned her, many times, about running in the woods. There had been reports of some young thugs making lewd suggestions to joggers. But that had been four or five months ago. Nobody had come forth lately with any complaints.

She had only started her run when she looked up to see her neighbor running towards here.

"Hi Samantha" Her neighbor, Frank Logan, called out. "Things are good?"

"Fine, Frank. How are you and Debbie doing?" She replied, as they passed one another.

"Fine, Samantha. You and Dave will have to come over and visit." He shouted back as he drew away.

"Okay Frank. Have Debbie give me a call." Samantha replied. She knew that Debbie would never call because Debbie weighed 190 pounds and was still eating everything in sight with both hooves. Debbie didn't like the contrasts she had to endure when she was in the company of slim ladies.

Samantha felt good and picked up her pace as she entered the wooded area. She felt close to nature running beneath the canopy of trees that shaded the path in front of her. In places the foliage of the trees was so thick it shrouded the path in darkness. She grew apprehensive as she approached what appeared to be a perfect spot for mugging.

Suddenly, a man who had been concealed behind a bush, stepped out right in front of her and blocked her path. He was so close to her she could smell the alcohol on his breath. Before she could react, he restrained her by holding a large knife against her breast. She froze and stopped instantly.

"Do you like living dangerously?" he asked as he pressed the knife against one breast and then the other.

"What do you want?" Samantha asked with an unconvincing air of authority that quickly wilted when be brought his knife up to her chin.

"That depends?" he growled.

"I have a few dollars. Here take them." Samantha pleaded as she reached out to hand him the money.

"We have time for more then that. Take off your ring and that pretty watch." He demanded and then continued. "What are you doing running out here in the wilderness? Do you know what happens to pretty women caught out here by people like me?" he inquired menacingly.

"Please let me go and I'll have my husband give you money; a lot of money. Please, just tell me how much you want."

"Lets not talk about money. Lets talk about what else you can give me. You're very attractive. Let's get off this path. Let's go." He demanded as he prodded her back into some dense bushes several feet away from the path. Once there, he told her to turn around.

Samantha immediately did what he asked. She was terrified. All kinds of options raced through her mind. He wasn't a very big man and he didn't look at all that robust. If she kicked him in the groin hard enough, she might be able to out run him. However, she was afraid if she bolted and he caught her, he would kill her. He had the knife and she knew she couldn't risk trying to wrestle it away from him. As long as he had the knife, Samantha realized that she was going to be the mouse in "the cat and mouse game" he wanted to play.

He moved closer to her and looked intently into her eyes. He appeared to be considering various alternatives. He was obviously enjoying his power over her. He reached out to her breast to remove her gold necklace. But Samantha stepped back. Her move infuriated him.

"Look Lady, you're not my guest. You're my prisoner. Do you understand? Do you know what prisoners do? Do you?" He hissed.

"They do what they're told." she whimpered.

"That's right; you're learning. And if you do exactly what I want you to do, you're going survive."

"Please don't hurt me. What do you want me to do?"

"I want you to play with this." He said, as his hand clutched his groin and then he undid his belt and let his pants drop to his ankles.

Realizing he couldn't run very fast with his pants dragging on the ground, she bolted. Instantly, he had his pants up. But, he dropped the knife before he plunged into the brush after her. She was only a few feet ahead of him when she stumbled and he fell on top of her. As they turned over and over; Samantha kicked and scratched him. Finally, he pinned her face down with one hand and with the other he grabbed the back of her jersey and pulled the neckline against her throat. But it tore and he fell backwards allowing her to briefly break free. As she tried to get up, he grabbed her shorts, by the waist band, and pulled her back down onto the ground and crawled on top of her. Desperate, Samantha started to scream.

"Shut up you bitch! Now I'm going to fuck you over good." He screamed, as he ripped off her torn jersey and threw it aside.

His strength surprised and horrified her. She realized, as he reached back and threatened to punch her, that he could easily kill her. She knew she couldn't flee nor fight. So, in order to survive; she accepted she would have to submit to his indecent demands.

"Please don't hit me; I'll do what you want. Please don't hurt me" She pleaded as he pulled her to her feet. She stood in front of him meekly with her arms hanging by her sides. He seemed pleased by her passive demeanor.

"That's better honey. Maybe we can get along after all." He said. "Now what's under here?" He whispered as he reached out with both hands and squeezed her breasts.

Samantha instinctively raised her hands to cover her breasts.

"Didn't you just say you weren't going to give me anymore grief? Do you want some of this?" He threatened as he pressed a fist against her jaw.

Samantha meekly dropped her hands to her sides.

"These are lovely. Why would you want to hide them?" He smirked, as he attempted to remove her bra.

"I've got my hands full." He sneered. "Reach down and get rid of your shorts. I don't want anything between us." He insisted, as he continued to tug at her bra.

Obediently, she reached down and released the string holding up her shorts and was about to slide them down over her hips when she heard someone rushing towards them through the bushes. Realizing help was imminent, she pushed him back with such force he stumbled to his knees just as a tall elderly man ran into the clearing.

"What's going on here?" Samantha's rescuer shouted.

Samantha's assailant answered boldly;

"She's my wife." Her assailant shouted out boldly. "She's giving me a hard time. Stay out of it or I'll kick your ancient ass."

"I'm not his wife. He's a lying bastard." Samantha screamed, as she rushed to the man's side, seeking his protection. Her assailant picked up a small log and swung it at the newcomer's head. But, he ducked and then knocked the assailant to the ground with a straight left jab to the assailant's chest.

Samantha's rescuer shouted. "Get out of here and get the police. I'll take care of Romeo if he wants to continue the fight."

Samantha pulled her bra back into place but refused to leave. "I'm not going anywhere until I'm sure you've got this bastard totally controlled."

As she spoke, her offender started to get up. Samantha picked up the log and stunned him with a blow along side his jaw.

"Okay lady, that's enough. Let's roll him over and we'll tie his hands behind his back. Get that jersey over there and tear it into two pieces." He urged, as he held the felon down. Samantha tore it apart and handed her rescuer the pieces.

"Okay now, sit on his shoulders." As she did, her rescuer tied the felon's hands together behind his back.

Satisfied he had him properly secured, he again urged Samantha to run for the police.

This time Samantha took off running as fast as she could. In a moment or so she reached the nearest house where she immediately began to pound on the front door. When a startled woman opened it, Samantha fell into her arms.

"Please call the Police." Samantha sobbed hysterically. "Some savage tried to rape me. He ripped off my shirt and had a stranger not come to my rescue, I could be dead right now, or I could have aids. Thank God he heard my screams, or I could be out there right now, being forced to do whatever that bastard wanted. I've never been so frightened in my life. I was paralyzed by fear. I'm so ashamed. I would have done anything to keep him from killing me. Please, could I use your bathroom? I think I'm going to throw up. Just thinking, about what he wanted me to do, is making me sick. Please, where is your bathroom?" Samantha pleaded and then added.

He has the bastard pinned to the ground. I don't know how long he can hold him."

The woman's husband immediately called 911 while his wife led Samantha to the bathroom. Left alone in the bathroom, Samantha looked in the mirror and suddenly her fear and anxiety was replaced by a fierce rage.

"That son of bitch, god damn him, if I ever get the chance, I'll kill the bastard. What he tried to do to me will haunt me forever, if I let it, and I'm not going to give that low life that satisfaction. I can't wait to testify against him. He's going to do time for what he tried to do to me."

Samantha's raging was interrupted by the lady of the house.

"Are you all right my dear?" The woman asked, as Samantha opened the bathroom door.

"I certainly am now. Thank you." Samantha said, as the woman handed her a clean blouse and attended to Samantha's scraps and bruises.

"Where do you live Ms.? I'm sorry, what is your name? Is there someone we can call?" The man of the house asked, when he put down the phone.

"I'm Samantha O'Connor and my husband and I live over on Collai Street. He's on a flight to England and won't get there until late tonight. I don't want him to know about this until he gets back. So please don't tell anyone about what happened. I have a lot of neighbors who might try and to inform him. I'm fine now, thanks to your wife. I'm sorry I can't thank you properly unless I know your name.

"I'm Bill and this is my wife Susan Hanrahan."

As Samantha finished thanking the Hanrahans, a policeman rapped on the front door.

"Excuse me folks. Are you the lady who was attacked in the woods?" The policeman asked, as he stared at Samantha.

"Yes; but please lets hurry. I only hope we're not too late. The man who helped me has my assailant tied up on the ground. We've got to hurry. Please hurry." Samantha urged, as she brushed by the policeman and moved quickly to the police car.

After thanking the Hanrahans, the policeman turned and followed Samantha. A second policeman opened the back door of the car to let Samantha enter the vehicle, while she continued to urge the police to hurry.

"Okay, lady; point the way!" One of the policemen ordered, as they entered the car.

"Straight ahead, to that stone gate" Urged, a pointing Samantha.

Once there, the two policemen and Samantha vaulted from the car and ran into the woods.

Arriving at the scene; they discovered Samantha's rescuer with his foot still on the neck of the prostrate thug.

One of the policemen recognized the assailant. As he pulled him to his feet he said: "Well look at who we've got here, you scumbag. It looks like you got your ass kicked by one tough old bird. I want to thank you, sir, for nailing this bastard. He's been getting away with beating up on people for years. But, this will be the last time; won't it Wilber? Hold your hands still while I fit these bracelets on you."

Wilber mumbled something about a cheap shot and then fell silent after the policeman read him his rights and told him to keep quiet.

As he was about to be lead off, Samantha poked her index finger into Wilber's face and demanded he return the jewelry he had taken from her.

"How am I going to do that you dumb bitch? Haven't you noticed where my hands are? Reach in my pockets yourself. But watch out for butch. He might spit all over your hand."

"Shut your mouth Wilber; or I'll stick this night stick down your throat." One of the policemen threatened. Then he turned to Samantha to ask her to describe her jewelry.

"Okay Wilber, what did you do with it?

"She's crazy. She offered it to me if I would do in her husband. I told her it was junk and threw it at her. She went off like a rocket and we got into it after she slapped me across the face. I tore her cheap jersey when I threw her to ground just to get away from her. She bounced right back up and ran after me yelling and screaming and tried to pull down her bra, I suppose, to make it look like I was trying to rape her. About that time, the old dude rushed up, and despite what I said, he cold cocked me. Then, she gave such a convincing 'damsel in distress performance', that I knew I couldn't possibly convince the old dude of what really happened. So, I just laid there and waited for you guys to show. I know it looks bad. But it's the truth. Check my record. You'll see I've never been even charged, let alone convicted of trying to do some woman against her will. I'm in high demand by the ladies. Now that I think about it, that's probably what this broad wanted"

"Wilber shut up. You'll have your day in court."

"Officer, does that mean I'll have to testify?" asked Samantha.

"Yes it does. That's the system and it's likely that it will be unpleasant for you. Wilber has had a lot experience hood winking juries. You'll no doubt have to undergo an ordeal by his defense lawyer."

After the officer finished speaking, he turned to his partner and asked him if he had found the knife. When his partner said no, a slight frown crossed his face. He then asked him if he had found the jewelry. The officer produced a baggie containing several pieces that he handed to Samantha which she identified as hers.

"I'll get these people out of here." The one policeman said to the other. "But, you'll have to stay and secure the scene until the lab people get here and search the area thoroughly. The existence of the knife is going to be critical to this case. If it's here, they'll find it."

On their way back to the police car, Samantha pondered what the policeman meant when he said; "If it's here........" Suddenly she felt an uneasiness in her stomach when she considered the consequences if the knife were not found.

When they arrived back at the police car, the policeman stuffed Wilber into the back seat of the car. As he did, a second police car drove up and a police sergeant got out. After a brief conversation between the policemen, the sergeant asked Samantha and her rescuer if they would come to the police station with him and file a criminal complaint. Both Samantha and her new friend agreed.

On the way to the police station, Samantha turned to the elderly gentleman that had saved her life.

"God I'm sorry. In all this confusion I never had the chance to introduce myself. I'm Samantha O'Connor and you are who?"

"My name is Desmond. Desmond Doyle"

"And Desmond, do you live here in Cartwheel Lake?"

"Yes I do, but I've only been here a couple of months. I'm originally from Calgary, Alberta."

"What brought you to New York?"

"Well, I'm a geologist. My management felt I was getting a little long in the tooth for the rigors of field work; so they promoted me to a soft job here at the head office. Although I loved field work; I knew they were right. The cold of winter in the wilderness is tough, even on a young man."

"Is there a Mrs. Doyle?" Samantha inquired; surprised by her own boldness.

"No there's not; I'm single."

"I have to ask this. But only, if you promise to forgive my curiosity."

"Of course, please ask."

"How did you learn to punch like that?"

"Well, Samantha, if you live in Calgary, you play hockey nine months of the year. And when you play hockey, you learn how to defend yourself. But enough about me. I'm very impressed with you. Most women who had endured the experience you just went through; would be under sedation. But here we are now, on our way to the police station, and it appears it was a piece of cake for you. Or, is your composure only skin deep?"

"I suspect, when I've had time to consider what might have happened, I'm going to wake up in the middle of some night in a cold sweat. A person never knows how they're going to perform in any crisis. Certainly, had you not come along when you did, I could now be dead. Just knowing that I would have gone down fighting; gives me a real shot of self esteem."

"As you know, Mrs. O'Connor, I'm a jogger too. If it would help your piece of mind, I'm available to jog with you. Usually, I leave my place around 5:30 in the morning. Of course, I can change my schedule if 5:30 is too early for you."

"Well, thank you Desmond. If you're free tomorrow, we can start running together in the morning."

"All I need to get to your place, Mrs. O'Connor, is your address and I'll be there tomorrow morning at 5:30."

"It's a date, Desmond. My name is Samantha and my friends call me Sam. You may call me Sam."

"Oh, I see we've arrived at the police station. I've never been in a police station. The building looks a little intimidating." Samantha observed, after a policeman opened the car door and motioned them to follow him.

Once in the building, they were met by a young attractive woman in civilian clothes who introduced herself as detective Molly Malone. She led Samantha and Desmond to a small room where she introduced them to detective John Deteadora, who explained that he would take Desmond's statement. Detective Malone then lead Samantha to a second interrogation room. Once inside the room, Detective Malone explained that female victims of a sex crime were always interviewed by a female detective.

Ms. Malone began by asking Samantha to state exactly what had happened. She then listened intently to Samantha's statement without making a single comment.

When Samantha finished Ms. Malone asked,

"How do you and your husband get along?"

A surprised Samantha asked. "What do you mean?"

"Do you still have sex regularly?" Ms. Malone asked.

"Is it essential, to the processing of my complaint, you pry into my personal life?"

"Mrs. O'Connor, you are going to be cross examined on the stand, under oath, by an aggressive attorney. What we really have here is a 'she said- he said' situation. The guy you are accusing, of attacking you, is an experienced felon and he's going to be very convincing on the stand. It's my job to get the facts and deliver them to the D.A. Now personally, I believe you. But my opinion, and that's all it is, an opinion, doesn't mean anything in a court of law. I want to point out to you, that in your story, you mention that your assailant prodded you several times with a large knife. Where is the knife? You don't seem to have any idea where the knife went. A second thing bothers me. What was a scumbag, like Wilber Coirpeach, doing in the woods at six A.M.? People like Wilber Coirpeach don't get up early unless they have a very good reason. Is it possible that your husband arranged, with Wilber, to dispose of you?"

"I don't think there's a remote possibility that my husband would hire someone to murder me. It's beyond my imagination. He may be difficult at times, but oh no, it's just not possible." Samantha replied forcefully as though offended by the question.

"Well, Mrs. O'Connor, you would be shocked at some of the things that husbands, and sometime wives, end up doing, if they're desperate enough. Now, is there a remote possibility that your husband might be involved with another woman?"

Samantha looked away from the detective and stared at the blank white walls of the room. She bit her lip, while she carefully considered the question.

"Yes, that's possible. But if he is, he has been damn careful for I haven't seen any indication"

"I understand your husband is somewhere in England. Before he left, did he seem to be behaving normally?"

"Now that you mention it, he did seem to be a little bit more pleasant than usual. But, it wasn't all that out of the ordinary."

"Let me ask you one final question. Do you have a friend that you're very fond of?"

"No I don't, detective. But like a lot women I know, there are times I would love to have one."

"Well, I think we've covered everything. But, I want you to think, very carefully, about the possibilities I've mentioned. If you think of anything, call me immediately. Again, as I said, I believe what you've told me and really do wish that I could help you. But, right now the only thing I can do is to prepare you for the courtroom. I think we're done here, unless you have thought of anything else. I'll walk you up front and we'll have a policeman drive you and Mr. Doyle home."

"Thank you very much, Ms Malone. If anything comes to mind, I'll call you immediately."

Samantha said very little as she and detective Malone walked up to the front desk of the police station. Her mind was so busy trying to recall all the details of her early morning conversation with her husband, that she hardly noticed all the activity going on in the building.

Detective Malone broke the silence when she asked the sergeant on duty to arrange transportation for Samantha and Desmond. The sergeant replied that Desmond was sitting in a police car out front waiting for Samantha.

Detective Malone escorted Samantha to the car and opened a rear door. Samantha got in and sat down beside Desmond in the back seat.

Desmond greeted her by asking how her interrogation session went.

"I have to be candid, I'm more upset now than I was after the attack this morning."

"What upset you Sam?" Desmond asked.

"Thinking about all the possibilities that detective Malone brought up."

"Like what?"

"Well, what happened to the knife? She feels that if it's not found, Wilber's attorney might crucify me on the stand. But how did your session go?"

"It was very short. Detective Deteadora scribbled a few notes in his little black book and asked me a couple questions and it was all over in less then ten minutes."

"What did you say to him?"

"I told him I heard a woman screaming and I rushed towards the sound and found you standing, with no blouse on, hovering over a man on his knees. The detective then asked who I thought was the aggressor. I told him I really wasn't sure but I assumed from your screaming that you were protecting yourself. He did not seem pleased. He went on to say that a good defense lawyer would be able to use my testimony to support the claims of the defendant."

"But Desmond, surely you saw him trying to remove my bra; didn't you?" Insisted Samantha;

"I'm sorry Samantha. You must have slapped his hands away just before I saw you."

"This trial thing could be a nightmare." Samantha exclaimed. "I don't like it. I could be in a lot of trouble if that the knife doesn't surface."

"I don't know Sam. But, you've got to trust the system. Let's talk about it in the morning, if we jog. You'll have had time to think over the whole experience and maybe something you've forgotten will pop up."

As Desmond finished speaking, the police car pulled up in front of Samantha's house.

"That's a good idea, Desmond. What time will you be here in the morning?"

"Somewhere close to 6 am. I'll call later this evening to see how you're doing. Talk to you then." Desmond promised. Then he shook her outstretched hand as she exited the vehicle.

"Thank you officer," Samantha called out, as she retreated up the sidewalk to the front door of her house.

Once inside, Samantha stripped off her clothes and showered. While toweling off, she began to go over the events of the day.

"Dave's comment about running in the woods was strange." She thought out loud. "It was a complete turn around of his past attitude. I wonder. Then, there was that mumbling about some kind of growing beast. It almost seemed like he was talking to his groin. He really is strange. I wish I had understood what he was saying… Probably not significant though; no matter what he meant."

Samantha suddenly felt very tired and instead of dressing, she crawled into bed and was soon in a deep sleep. Several hours later, during a terrifying dream, she was jarred awake by the incessant clanging of her bedroom phone. She looked at the caller ID display and when she saw it was Desmond, she answered it.

"Hi Des; how are you?" She cooed. Surprised that she had, she thought to herself. "Why did I do that?"

"Hi Sam, I wont keep you long. I just called to make sure you were okay."

"I'm fine Des. Your call woke me up."

"I'm sorry." Desmond claimed.

"Please don't be. I'm as hungry as a toothless tiger. Had you not called, I would have starved to death in my sleep."

"Well; I won't keep you. I'll see you around six tomorrow morning. Can I say I'm looking forward to seeing you?"

"Certainly you can and I confess to similar feelings. Good night. See you in the morning."

"Good night Sam." He said, as he hung up the phone.

"Samantha, I think you have a crush on Desmond." Samantha mused, as she put down the phone and reached for her robe.

After finishing a light meal, she sat down in front of her television set and waited to hear from Dave. At nine o'clock she decided Dave wasn't going to call; so she called it a night. After setting her alarm clock for five a.m., she crawled into bed. But, she couldn't sleep. She went over and over the possibility of her husband hiring someone to murder her. She would convince herself that it was not possible. But, after a few minutes, her doubt about her husband's innocence would resurface and she would have to struggle with the issue again. Finally, she drifted off only to be rudely awakened by a persistent rattle from her alarm clock.

She was surprised to find she was not tired. She suspected her desire to see Desmond had something to do with how she felt. She dressed quickly and was ready for Desmond's arrival long before six A.M. To her surprise, Desmond knocked on her door fifteen minutes before six o'clock. Apparently, he too was anxious for them to get together.

"Good morning Desmond. You're early. I didn't expect you so soon. But I'm happy you're here." Samantha gushed.

Desmond looked her over and smiled. Then, almost as an after thought, he asked her if she were ready.

When she answered affirmatively, they started off briskly. They had only run a few hundred feet when Desmond asked if Samantha wanted to run in the woods.

"Yes, lets. I've got to face that challenge eventually, so it might as well be now."

Once in the woods, they soon came to the spot where the attack had occurred. To their surprise the police had the area cordoned off.

"Let's look for it now." Samantha urged.

"We can't do that Sam. It's a crime scene. We'll not be able to search for the knife until the police give up their search. You have to be patient. Remember, there's a good possibility that they'll find the knife."

"Okay Des. But I didn't tell you what else detective Malone suggested."

"What was that Sam?"

"She interpreted the facts that she was aware of, as clearly indicating that Wilber Coirpeach was a paid hit man. Ms. Malone says Wilber's insisting that I met him out in the woods, to arrange for him to murder my husband and that we quarreled when I tried to buy his services with my jewelry. He also claims that he rejected my jewelry as being worthless and threw it at me, which prompted me to slap him across the face."

"How did he explain that you had no jersey on when I arrived on the scene?"

"He claimed he tore it off me when he was trying to get away from me."

"That's a stretch."

"Maybe so. But Ms Malone is fearful of what Wilber's attorney will do to me when he gets me on the stand. She pointed out that Wilber has had all kinds of experience dealing with juries. If he can get the jury to believe him, he's only guilty of listening to a proposition to murder someone and he'll walk. If the jury believes me, he's going down for attempted murder. Ms Malone is convinced that someone hired him to murder me. I tend to agree with her. But the only person that would have a motive is my husband, Dave. And Dave would only want me dead if he had a replacement on the shelf waiting to share his sack. But, Dave has never given me any reason to believe that he has a "friend". Of course, the old saw about the wife being "the last to know" has a history of being true."

"God Sam, we've got to find that knife." Desmond exclaimed. "If we don't, the barbarian, like you say, may walk. One thing I don't think you have to fear is being prosecuted for hiring a hit man. If the D.A. has a modicum of sense, it won't happen."

"Of course, I don't know the D.A. Desmond. But, if he's at all objective, I think I'm okay. However, if the press gets a hold of the story, all bets will be off." Samantha concluded.

Since their conversation gave them both a lot to think about, they spoke very little the rest of the run. When they arrived back at Samantha's house, they found a police car parked out in front. As they approached the vehicle, Ms. Malone and another person got out of the vehicle.

"How're you doing?" Ms. Malone asked. With out waiting for a reply, she continued. "I would like you to meet one of our electronic technicians; Bill Hernanez." Bill nodded as Ms. Malone continued; "This is Samantha O'Connor and Desmond Doyle. With your permission, Samantha, Bill is going to install a recorder on your phone. When your husband calls, we'll record everything he says and later we'll do a voice stress analysis of what he says. If he lies about anything we'll detect it."

"Well Ms Malone, I don't understand how such a device works. But you certainly can install it on my phone. Dave hasn't called. But I expect to hear from him within the next couple hours. How long will it take to install it, Mr. Hernanez?"

"I'll have operating it in less than 5 minutes Mrs. O'Connor. If you don't want to record a conversation, you will be able to shut the device off. However, I would suggest that you leave it on continuously. It's easy to forget to turn it on, particularly if you are under stress when you get a critical call."

After Desmond departed, Samantha ushered Ms. Malone and Bill Hernanez into the house. Samantha and Ms. Malone went into the living room and sat down. And while Bill Hernanez installed the recorder, Ms Malone asked Samantha if she could recall anything peculiar that her husband had said or done lately.

Samantha told Ms. Malone about Dave changing his attitude about her running in the woods and about his mumbling something gross about a growing beast. Ms Malone thought that Dave's reference to a growing beast might be important and urged Samantha to try and recall what he might have been saying. Samantha assured Ms. Malone that she had been doing just that for almost twenty four hours. Ms. Malone smiled, and then said they might have a break in the case and began to elaborate.

"Our search team has found a cell phone. It hasn't been exposed to the elements and we're checking now to see who it might belong to. If it's Wilber's phone, and we think it is, a record of his calls may lead us to who hired him to harass you. In any event, I'll keep you posted."

As Ms. Malone finished speaking, Bill Hernanez called from the other room to say he had completed the installation. After assuring Samantha that every thing was all set, they left.

Samantha watched the two of them walk to their car. She thought about how fortunate she was to have someone as gracious and competent as Molly Malone in her camp. She wondered why such a beautiful young woman would want to be a police woman. "Oh, what I would give to have her beautiful black hair." Samantha mused.

She turned from the door and caught a glimpse of herself. "It's time to get dressed." she declared.

A half an hour later, after having finished dressing, she returned to the hall mirror. Satisfied with what she had accomplished, she smiled into the mirror and declared; "And you thought it couldn't be done; shame on you."

Suddenly her reverie was interrupted by the chimes from her cell phone. She stared at the display. It was an overseas call. Her assurance plummeted. She let it ring. She thought to herself; let it ring, let the bastard call back. Then, she chastised herself for rushing to a judgment. The phone went silent. She squeezed it in her hand and for some strange reason, she couldn't put it down.

As she sat there, events in her life with Dave paraded through her mind. She remembered their first date and what a gentleman he had been. Then there were the many dinners at the home of his parents. She had loved them and was devastated by their untimely deaths. The party, oh the party; the night we celebrated Dave's promotion. Dave drank too much and I had to put him to bed and lie there beside him thinking; so this is what vice presidents wives do. Her mind drifted away from days gone by. She recalled Henri Poincare's summation of life; 'Our thoughts, our concerns, our loves, and our hates are only gleams in the midst of a long night. But, it is the gleam that is everything.'

Then the phone vibrated in her hand and began to chime; it was Dave again. "Hello Dave; how was the flight?"

"Is that you Sam? I wondered what happened to you when you didn't answer my earlier call. Are you okay?

"I'm fine Dave. How was the flight?"

"You just asked me that Sam."

"I know Dave but you didn't answer. So how was the flight?

"Routine, I dozed most of the way. Where did you jog?"

"Oh, the usual"

"Where's the usual, in the woods?" Dave persisted.

"No; around the lake" Samantha countered.

"That's not the usual. What are you trying to say?" Dave replied, with a voice laced with irritability.

"Hey Dave, when did my jogging route become so goddamn important? What am I missing here?"

"I'm sorry, Sam. Yesterday was a bad day. The stay over in Gander was much longer than usual. The whole thing was exhausting. But I just couldn't get back to sleep, once I woke up. Tomorrow's going to be a tough day. The British have a number of contentious issues they'll want resolved before they jump into bed with us on the Iceland project. But, the one in Russia will be particularly difficult to resolve.

Anyway, I'm going to try and get a couple more hours sleep. I'll let you go and I'll call you in a couple of days."

"That's fine, Dave. I'll talk to you then. I hope your day goes well. Good bye."

Samantha put the phone down and mumbled to herself. "That's the first time in twenty years I haven't ended a conversation with him by saying 'I love you.' And he didn't even notice. I'm afraid the hand writing is on the wall. He's probably got her with him in some fancy hotel in London. It could be worse. I could have a bunch of teenage kids causing me grief."

Samantha pulled Ms. Malone's card from her pocket and dialed her number.

"Detective Malone, how can I help you?"

"Hi Molly; I've got a recording here for you to study. I just got off the phone with Dave. He sure was preoccupied with where I jogged."

"I'm on my way, Samantha. I'll see you in fifteen minutes."

"Thanks Molly."

Samantha felt empty as she verbalized her feelings.

"God, how could he? What kind of problems do we have that he would do such a desperate thing? What's he done? I wonder if he has financial problems. Supporting two women could be expensive. He has been traveling overseas a lot. Could he be into drugs? I just can't imagine what kind of problems could drive him to murdering his wife."

Samantha's thoughts were interrupted by Molly Malone ringing the door bell.

"Thank you for coming, Molly." Samantha said, as she opened the door and led Ms. Malone into the living room.

"How did it go, Samantha?"

"I'll let you listen to the tape." Samantha said, as she motioned towards the recorder.

Ms. Malone picked up the recorder, pushed the play button, and listened intently as the machine played back the tape.

"I'm sorry, Sam, but I don't think you need an analyzer to tell you his hands are not clean."

"Needless to say, Molly, we're in total agreement. Ever since I hung up the phone, I've asked myself; what could possibly have driven him to such an action? I've lived with the man for over twenty five years. And it turns out I didn't know him at all."

"Samantha; don't blame yourself. Events can destroy anyone of us. It won't be long before we find what kind of trouble he's in. Do you have any idea?"

"Molly; I don't have a clue. Where do we go from here? Do you think he'll try and call Wilber Coirpeach?"

"I don't think so, Sam. He's got to know that he can't use his cell phone. But, he may try calling from a public phone. That would be very awkward. If he's got a 'friend' with him, he may try using her cell phone. By the way, the cell phone we have does belong to Wilber. If anyone calls from England, we'll have their identity almost immediately."

"But, Molly, he has no pressing reason to call Wilber. As far as he knows, nothing happened in the woods. Why would he try and reach Wilber?"

"What he does will probably depend on how much pressure he's under. If he's in real trouble, he may want to contact Wilber only to assure him that you'll eventually be running in the woods. He may want to avoid the danger of making arrangements to hire a new hit man. Instinctively, I feel he's going to call and if he does, it's another indication that he's in very serious trouble.

I have to leave. But, I would like you to continue to try and come up with a reason for his behavior and if you do; call me immediately"

Their meeting over, Samantha walked Ms. Malone to the front door while still continuing to express her puzzlement at her husband's behavior. As she started down the front steps, Ms. Malone turned and said to Samantha; "We are all human, even your husband, and we all have our dark sides. Good bye Sam." And she was gone.

23

CHAPTER TWO

The next morning, while showering, Samantha heard her phone ringing. Reluctantly, she decided to let her answering machine record the message. Minutes later, she emerged from the bathroom and hurried to the machine. After activating it, she listened intently.

"Samantha." A female voice began. "A brief message came in on Wilber Coirpeach's cell phone. It was from one Susan Selkerk who called from London, England. The message read; 'Are you still available?'

Have you ever heard of a Susan Selkerk? Give me a call as soon as you can. It's Molly Malone."

"Susan Selkerk." Samantha mused. "Susan Selkerk; no I've never heard the name before. Susan Selkerk; no I'm certain."

Still searching her memory, she picked up the phone and dialed Molly's number.

"Good morning. Malone here, how can I help you?"

"Good morning, Molly. It's Samantha O'Connor. I just read your message. I'm certain, I've never heard of Susan Selkerk."

"Well anyway Sam, we've got Scotland Yard looking into who she might be. I'll let you know what they find. By the way, the technicians weren't able to find the knife."

"Well Molly, that knife's real. I can close my eyes and see every detail of it. It has to be there. Can you ask your technicians to repeat the search?" Samantha pleaded.

"Can't do Sam; technicians don't like their findings being challenged by non technical people.

"Can I take Desmond out there and search for it?"

"You can Sam. But remember, and this is important. If you find it, don't touch it. Call me immediately. Remember; it's evidence and if you find it, we don't want some wise-ass attorney suggesting that you tampered with it.

Anyway, I have to run. As soon as Scotland Yard gets back to us, I'll let you know what they found. Talk, to you later."

Samantha hung up the phone, looked at the clock and thought out loud: "It's about 3 o'clock in the afternoon, in England. I wonder if the wily banker will call today?"

Samantha sat down on the coach and let her mind review her life with Dave. She mostly recalled the happy times and there had been many. Then she decided not to waste any further time brooding about the past. Her future and what to do about it was the challenge now. She decided that if Dave was as guilty as it now appears their relationship was over. Then she thought. Maybe his actions could be explained? But after a few moments consideration, she resolved that she would accept reality and get on with her life and the hell with Dave.

It was at that moment, it dawned on her. A little over a year ago Dave had increased the insurance on her life.

"God! How could I've forgotten? I know he increased it; but I have no idea how much. Well, I can find out with a simple phone call. It had to be a substantial amount because the physical was extremely thorough. What was that agent's name? Martin, I think it was"

Samantha spent the next hour searching for Mr. Martin's card. Growing frustrated, she pulled too hard on a drawer in one of Dave's cabinets causing it to come loose from its runners. The contents lay scattered on the floor. As she gathered them to put back into the drawer; she noticed a copy of Synge's Playboy of the Western World. There hidden between the book's hard cover and its dust jacket was Bruce Martin's card.

"Bruce Martin, of course, I remember him. He was a very nice person. What an appropriate book for a philanderer to pick as a hiding place." She mused.

She looked at the clock. It was just after ten A.M. She thought; "He's probably in his office. I might as well get this over with now." She concluded, as she dialed the number on the card.

After few rings, a female voice said: "Bruce Martin's Insurance. I'm Sherry. How can I help you?"

Samantha introduced herself to Sherry and explained what she wanted to know. Sherry, then put Samantha on hold, after promising to return with the requested information.

Moments later, Sherry came back on line. "I'm sorry, Mrs. O'Connor, but your husband has a security lock on your policy."

"What's a 'security lock?" Samantha inquired politely.

"It simply means we, at your husband's request, cannot give out any information on your policy to anyone."

"Does that include me?" Samantha asked.

"I'm sorry, Mrs. O'Connor, it does. What I would suggest; is that I have Bruce call you when he gets back to the office."

"When will that be, Sherry?"

"Sometime tomorrow morning; would you like me to ask him to call you?" Sherry repeated.

"Yes Sherry; that will be fine. Thank you."

As soon as she cradled the phone, the obvious occurred to her.

"Dave has got to have a copy of the policy. But where would he hide it? God; it could be anywhere. It's got to be in his safe. But hell, I don't know the combination of the lock."

As she spoke, Samantha walked into Dave's study and over to his wall mounted strong box. She half heartily tugged on the combination lock securing it. As she expected, it held fast. She studied the lock carefully and observed it was a 'Master' lock.

"I recall someone talking the other day about deciphering the combination of a 'Master' lock. I'll ask Desmond if he has ever heard about it. Hell, I can get a bolt cutter and open it myself. But, I had better run that idea by Molly, before I do anything. I've got to face it; I'm on my own now. I'll just do a search myself, on the internet, to see if I can find any information about deciphering combination locks."

Samantha turned on her computer and after searching "combination locks" was delighted to find a procedure on how to obtain the combination of 'Master' locks. She printed out the procedure and studied it carefully. Satisfied she understood it, she pulled up a chair to the safe, sat down, and began applying the procedure. Two hours later, after many tries, she entered yet another combination. To her surprise and delight, when she pulled on the lock; it opened. She jotted down the three numbers of the combination on the instruction sheet she had being using.

She didn't immediately open the safe. She decided that she would reward herself, for her accomplishment, by having lunch. As she sat at her kitchen table she happened to glance at the combination. It was 6-21-8. She immediately teared up and began to cry for June 21, 1980 was their wedding day. She was still sobbing quietly when the phone started ringing 20 minutes later. When she saw it was Molly Malone she quickly regained her composure and picked up the phone.

"Hi Molly: What's happening?"

"Scotland Yard just called. They interviewed Susan Selkerk. She told them that she had been talking on her cell phone, in Harrods, when a well dressed man approached her and offered her 50 pounds to use her cell phone to make an emergency call to the States. According to her, she had just decided not to buy an expensive purse when he approached her and made his offer. The temptation was too great for her to resist because she really wanted the purse; so she let him use her cell phone. Now they need a picture of Dave. If I come by, can you provide me with one?" Without waiting for a reply Molly continued.

"Sam, you sound like you may be having a bad day. Now I don't want you to get too excited about this. But, Scotland Yard told me they don't think the lady is going to be able to identify a picture of your Dave. You know how the British police are; well I guess you don't. But, they don't speculate. I suspect they're on to something and as soon as they get to the bottom of it, they'll let us know all the details. Anyway, I'll be by shortly. See you then."

Samantha hung up the phone and immediately started searching for a picture of Dave. When she found one, she left it on the dinning room table along with an envelope, and then returned to the safe in Dave's office. Once there she reached out tentatively and opened the safe. After leafing through several various documents she finally found her life insurance policy. She wasn't sure why, but the amount of the policy pleased her, for it was for only a hundred thousand dollars. The date of the policy coincided with the date of her physical. She shuffled through the rest of the documents. But, she found nothing alarming. Dave's policy was there and it was for a million dollars; the amount that they both had agreed upon many years ago.

Finished searching, she piled all the documents up in the order she had found them and then put them back into the safe and snapped the lock closed. She felt relieved that she had not cut the lock open with a bolt cutter.

She was about to call Sherry, at Bruce Martin's, when Molly pulled up in the driveway in her unmarked police car. Samantha opened the door for her before she could push the door bell.

"Hi Molly; will this photograph do?" Samantha asked, as she handed the photo to Ms. Malone.

Molly studied it and then asked Samantha if she could use her computer to transmit it to Scotland Yard. Samantha agreed immediately, but warned Molly that she had no idea how to transmit anything, anywhere. Molly simply said; "Do you have a scanner? If you do, let me see your computer."

Samantha led Molly to her husband's office and motioned her to sit down at the computer. Molly complied and after getting Dave's system operational, she shortly had his image on its way to

London. Finished, she turned to Samantha and asked if she wanted the computer shut off. Samantha nodded yes. After Molly had shut the system down, she rose from the chair and walked towards the front door. As she did, she said to Samantha; "This whole case is getting very complicated. Your husband may not be as culpable as we thought. I'm anxious to hear what Scotland Yard has discovered. We should know that maybe as early as tomorrow. Anyway Sam, I've got to run. I'll call you as soon as I have anything new."

Ms. Malone gone, Samantha picked up the phone and dialed Bruce Martin's number. When Sherry answered, Samantha told her that she had found a copy of the policy. Then she asked Sherry if there was more than one policy. When Sherry said no, Samantha told her she no longer needed to talk to Mr. Martin.

After hanging up the phone, she turned on a television news program. She listened intently as a talking head complained about how America's bankers had almost destroyed the world's financial system and that ultimately, he claimed, they must be made to pay for their crimes.

Starting a conversation with the television set Samantha cried out; "I've got a banker you can roast in hell for me."

The talking head continued advocating immediate and severe punishment for all top executives of large U.S. banks. He finished his diatribe by describing a particularly hard case that involved Chekhov, a small city near Moscow, in Russia. Apparently, the city had been sold a huge amount of worthless mortgaged backed securities. The city was so pressed for cash it had to cancel a planned trip of its mayor to its twin city in New York State. However, the city apparently had enough cash to buy the services of a collection agency that uses questionable tactics to collect debt and gets very good results.

The commentator appeared to relish the thought of some rogue U.S. banker having to deal with a collection agency from Russia named Intimidator Inc.

Samantha hadn't been listening too closely to the television set. But, when she heard the word "intimidator", her interest suddenly soared. She had just seen a brochure of a company by that name in Dave's office safe. Immediately, she rushed to the safe, opened it, and found the brochure. Sure enough, it was the Russian Company the television commentator had been talking about.

Samantha sat down and opened the brochure. On its front page its blazing logo proclaimed; "If you owe a client of Intimidator Inc. money, you'll pay it back in one coin or another." The rest of the brochure listed the various methods the company would use to get their client's money back. Essentially, they were boasting about how proficient they were in the use of intimidation.

After finishing with the brochure, Samantha put it back in the safe. As she did, she wondered if Dave were involved with Intimidator Inc. If he is, she concluded, he might be in a lot of trouble. Later, as she lay in bed, she wondered if Wilber Coirpeach's attack on her may have been orchestrated by Intimidator Inc. to terrorize Dave. The more she thought about it the more she liked her idea.

Just before she fell asleep, she said out loud: "I must run the idea by Molly first thing in the morning." Pleased she drifted off.

CHAPTER THREE

It was almost 6 a.m. Samantha had been sitting in her front room for ten minutes staring out the window, lost in thought, when Desmond ran into her view. Before he could reach her front door, she opened it and greeted him. "Good morning Desmond. How're you doing this morning?" She inquired.

"I'm fine Sam; are you ready to go?"

"Yes and no. Can we walk first before we jog? I would like to discuss the knife and its whereabouts."

"Sure. What's the latest on it, Samantha?"

"Molly Malone called yesterday and said they could not find the knife and the search has been canceled. I protested. But she claimed the decision was final. I asked if you and I could search the area. She said we could, but added a caveat. If we find the knife, she warned, that we're not to touch it."

"That's understandable, Samantha. No one can prove anything with corrupted evidence." Desmond concurred and then continued. "Let's start where you last saw it."

"I remember, Desmond, he had the knife in his right hand when he unbuckled his belt. When his pants hit the ground, I bolted. When he caught up with me, he didn't have the knife and I never saw it again."

"I don't know if it will help, Sam. But, why don't you describe every detail about the knife that you can remember."

"Well, the blade looked like it might have been made out of a dark gray aluminum but it wasn't shiny." Samantha paused and bit her lower lip.

"Go on Sam; what else do you remember? Did anything standout about its cutting edges or its length?"

"Yes, I remember them clearly. The top edge was serrated and the bottom had a "V" shaped notch cut out of it. I remembered being terrified by its seven or eight inch length. Oh, and its menacing blade extended back about an inch beyond its black plastic handle."

Sam, I think you're describing a scuba diver's knife. Most of them are made out of titanium which resembles aluminum. But unlike aluminum, titanium doesn't corrode in salt water. It also has a couple other properties that might explain why the police haven't found it."

"Like what kind of properties?" A curious Samantha asked.

"Titanium's non magnetic and a poor conductor of electricity, which would make it difficult to find with a metal detector."

"Do you think it being a diver's knife might be important?" Samantha asked.

"I don't really have any idea what might be important. I just know from watching 'Law and Order' and other similar shows that the police regard such details as being important." Desmond shrugged.

Samantha didn't continue the conversation for she had begun to look for the site which was no longer marked by bright yellow security tape. They shortly concluded they had found the spot and began their search. However, after thrashing about in the damp underbrush for twenty minutes or so, Desmond suggested they would need something like ground radar if they were going to continue the search. After discussing it briefly, they decided to postpone further searching until they had obtained some kind of more sophisticated metal detecting equipment.

Back jogging, Samantha noticed that Desmond seemed almost disinterested in the search. She wondered if he knew something she didn't know. Maybe, she concluded, he thought she had imagined the knife? Perhaps that was why he had asked her describe the knife. Then she thought; he sure seemed to know a lot about knifes used by scuba divers. His attitude surprised her for she felt she had been very convincing when she had described the knife. Arriving back at her house, Samantha put the knife out of her mind, bid Desmond goodbye, and entered her house. Once inside, she strained to hear a beep from her answering machine. But, she heard only a disappointing silence. After breakfast and a long soak in the bathtub, she dressed casually and sat down on her living room sofa. She was about to turn on the television when she noticed a copy of the 'Playboy of the Western World' sitting on the chair next to her. She picked up the book and after reading the introduction, she thought Christy Mahon, the sly central character in the book, would have done well selling mortgage backed securities to trusting investors. As she put down the book, the phone began to ring. She looked at the caller I.D. screen and read Dave's name. Immediately, she answered it.

"Hi Dave, how are things in London?" Samantha queried, lightly.

"Hi Sam, not good, the Brits are wary of our Iceland scheme. I'm liable to be here for God knows how long. I can't find a single banker here in London that trusts anybody. Money is just not moving and if it doesn't start to get legs soon, we'll be up to our derrieres in deflation."

"Is deflation that bad, Dave?" "It's very bad, Sam. When you have deflation, the value of the money you have grows. You have less incentive to spend it. The longer you delay a purchase, the lower the real price will be when you eventually buy. The gross effect of deflation slows the circulation of money while suppressing the volume of trade. It makes the servicing of debt ever more onerous. Tax revenues decline dramatically and if government fails to introduce proper corrective legislation, the result is depression. Even a small amount of deflation could very quickly destabilize the mortgage back derivative industry. Just the threat of deflation has made it very difficult to sell derivatives. Now the only way you can move them is to give them away to the unwary as Christmas gifts. But enough of my problems; how are you doing? Are you jogging?"

"Yes, I'm running with an elderly neighbor. He's a very nice fellow and I enjoy his company. So if you're not back soon, don't worry. My new friend looks like he could keep me happy for awhile." Samantha teased.

"I'm glad you've found someone to frolic with, if that's the appropriate verb." Dave responded, in kind, to Samantha's quip. Sensing her husband's mood to be reasonable, Samantha decided to bring up the Intimidator Inc. issue again.

"Yesterday," Samantha began, "the television news featured a financial guy who was very upset with bankers who had peddled toxic assets to trusting municipalities around the world. He went on and on about a Russian city that had purchased a lot of them. The city is now broke and can't meet its payroll. Anyway, in desperation, the city fathers hired a collection agency that calls itself; Intimidator Inc. The company appears to be little more than a gang of extortionists and their tactics are brutal. The commentator went on to say that they have been mainly harassing American banking executives in an effort to recover losses. What concerned me was the attitude of the commentator. He felt that the American bankers were getting their just returns. The situation concerns me. Are these people leaning on anyone you know?" Samantha paused and waited. When a minute passed and Dave hadn't responded she asked him if he was still there. Finally he replied.

"They haven't contacted you, have they?" He asked in a strained voice.

Annoyed Samantha demanded to know what was going on. Dave ignored her question and claimed something had come up and he would call her back tomorrow. Despite her objections, he broke off the conversation by hanging up the phone. Samantha sat looking at the phone in her hand while she considered all the possibilities that might explain her husband's strange behavior. Obviously, he was mixed up with the Intimidator Inc. people. She wondered; could they be involved somehow with the attack on her? As she thought about that possibility, the phone began to ring. She looked at the I.D. screen; it was Molly Malone.

"Hi Molly; how are you doing?"

"I've got news, Samantha. Susan Selkerk turned out to be the wife of a magistrate. She's positive that the man that asked to use her cell phone was not your husband. She also added that she thought he might have had a slight Slavic accent." After a sigh of relief, Samantha brought up her phone conversation with Dave. After discussing it thoroughly with Molly; they agreed that Dave might well be involved, somehow, with agents of Intimidator Inc. After both of them had considered the ramifications of such a possibility Molly brought up another disturbing issue.

"Well I have more news. The District Attorney feels that the case against Wilber is too weak, without the knife, to risk going to trial. He wants us to continue the investigation. Now if we find that Intimidator Inc. is involved, we'll try to get a judge's approval to convene a grand jury. I'm concerned. If they don't rule to go to trial, Wilber Coirpeach will walk."

"You can't be serious. He damn near killed me and had Desmond not arrived, he would have raped me."

"Samantha, you've got to accept that without the knife, we can't convict him."

"What about Desmond's testimony?"

"What testimony? He saw the two of you fighting?"

"I know that's what he said. But, how can anyone take the word of a convicted felon against the word of a woman who had been stripped of half her clothes and threatened with rape?"

"Samantha, I'm not the jury. I know you're telling the truth because I trust my intuition. But in a court of law, only the facts rule. The first thing his attorney is going to say is: "Where's the knife?" Then, he'll say something cute like; 'You can't slice without the knife.' I think you and I have to discuss every possibility of what happened to it. Let's just suppose that Wilber and Desmond are in this thing together. The knife has disappeared. Who had an opportunity to dispose of it? Clearly, Desmond did. He had Wilber contained for the police. But if they're in it together, there's one explanation for what happened to that knife. What do you really know about Desmond?"

"Well Molly, it's like you say; I trust my intuition. I feel strongly he's genuine. But, if he isn't, I'll never trust my intuition again. One thing, though, I'm absolutely certain of. That knife was there."

"I'm certain it was, Sam, and with any luck we're going to find it."

Buoyed by Molly's moral support, Samantha expressed her appreciation to Molly and bid her goodnight.

CHAPTER FOUR

It had been twenty minutes since Dave O'Connor had hung up the phone. But Samantha's question; "Are these people leaning on anyone you know?" still plagued him because he didn't know how to answer it. How could he admit that Intimidator Inc. had every moral right, to harass him? He had sold worthless mortgage backed securities to the city of Chekhov. Worse yet, he knew they were worthless when he sold them. He had used all the old excuses like; business is business, to assuage his conscience. Now, he felt sick in the stomach. His immorality had been broadcast to the country by the six o'clock news. But, what really shamed him was knowing it wasn't what he had done that bothered him; but that he had been caught doing it.

He looked down at the letter that had come in the morning's post. Its multicolored bold letterhead read; Intimidator Inc. He picked up the letter and reread it aloud very slowly.

Dear Mr. David R. O'Connor:

The people of the City of Chekhov will be sore pressed to survive the coming Russian winter. They have no funds to provide for their needy. Simply put, people will freeze to death in the streets and in their homes. If the coming tragedy occurs, you will be one of the people who could have done something to have averted it. On your conscience will be the agonizing death of many people.

Your intimate friends like Ms. Elizabeth Foster, here in England, and your other dear friend in the States, Mrs. Charles Van Cleve, will be very proud of you for any contribution you make to the fund that we, here at Intimidator Inc., are creating for the people of Chekhov.

If you can be available Wednesday next, we would like to meet with you in room 1122 of the Cavendish Hotel, at 7 p.m. to discuss your tentative contribution to the Chekhov Fund.

Ivan Turgenev

Dave put down the letter and shaking his head said aloud: "How the hell did they find out about Libby and Frances? Christ, I've only dealt Libby 5 or 6 times. Well, maybe more. What am I thinking? I must have screwed her at least that many times the week we spent in Scotland. She knows how to shift gears. I'm about to get my balls blown off and I'm counting the number of times I rammed a tart. She's not a problem. It's Fran I'm worried about.

"I told you." Dave chided, as he stared down at his groin. "You weren't smart. One doesn't mess with the CEO's wife. But, you insisted. I guess I'll never learn. You just can't be allowed to do my thinking.

God, I'm in trouble. They're going to want a hell of hunk of change. Where am I going to get it? Libby's out of the picture. Maybe I can put the squeeze on Fran. I like that thought. She sure has been great in the sack. She might want to help. Yea sure; she'll want to help push me under a semi. If it's over, what a ride it has been!

What am I going to do with the broom lady? I don't know how she'll react. But, she could straighten my intestines with one of her brooms. I can close my eyes and see the witch staring at me pretending she's suffering terribly while savoring the opportunity to destroy me financially. The more I think about it, the worse it gets. Oh the hell with it, I need distraction!"

Dave put the letter down; sat down in an easy chair; turned on the television set and in twenty minutes was sound asleep.

The next few days were consumed by meetings with customers that were largely a waste of time. Then came the fateful Wednesday and Dave was ushered into room 1122 of the Cavendish Hotel.

"Good evening, Mr. O'Connor. I'm Ivan Torgenev and as you know, I represent Intimidator Inc. I want to thank you for coming here tonight."

Dave shook Mr Turgenev's extended hand. Dave immediately was struck by how much Ivan Turgenev looked like Vladimir Putkin. He had to be a couple of inches short of six feet tall. He appeared to be mild mannered and very confident of himself. Dave was not surprised when he got right to the issue.

"As our letter explained, Mr. O'Connor, we are most anxious for you to make a contribution to our Chekhov fund. The people of Chekhov need from you a million dollars which means we need you to give one million for the people of Chekhov and two hundred thousand dollars for our commission. We would like the money within thirty days." Torgenev paused and waited patiently for Dave's response.

Dave thought to himself. "Hell it could have been a lot worse. I can probably raise that in a couple of weeks without Samantha finding out what's going on. If I can get Frances to help, it might not be a problem at all. I'll see if I can negotiate the tag down."

"Well Mr Putkin-I'm sorry… Mr. Turgenev. But you do strongly resemble the Prime Minister."

"Please don't be embarrassed." He replied graciously. "I'm an admirer of our Premier. You have paid me a great compliment, thank you, Mr.O'Connor. But, now back to business. Can you agree to our request or do you need time to arrange for the funds?"

"Well, it seems like a steep penalty to have to pay for a legitimate business deal gone wrong. I could maybe agree to something around six hundred thousand. One point two million is out of the question." Dave asserted.

"Well Mr. O'Connor, we had thought you would have appreciated our offer because we both know that what you did to the city fathers of Chekhov was unconscionable. You knew the derivatives were worthless and you knew that you were taking advantage of a desperately poor city. We thought our offer generous considering how unethical your conduct. It's our policy that when a generous offer is countered, we normally increase our demand by ten percent. But, since you have not done business with us before, I'll suspend that policy and leave our offer as stated. However, I repeat, counter offers are normally discouraged. It is now your move Mr. O'Connor."

When Mr. Turgenev finished speaking, he sat back in his chair, relaxed and stared out the window at the city of London.

Dave knew his position was untenable. But, he delayed his response merely to save face. After a minute or so, he agreed to the price.

Mr. Turgenov congratulated him on his decision. After they agreed to where and when the money would be paid, both Dave and Mr. Turgenev rose to their feet, shook hands and parted.

On his way back to his hotel, Dave mused at how more than a million dollars had been plucked from his pocket and not one threat had been used. And then, almost amused, he observed that intimidation can be a subtle thing when done by a gentleman.

As Dave entered his Hotel room, he turned on his computer. While it warmed up, he used the bathroom and while doing so, he stared into the mirror and said out loud;

"It's now time to compose an email masterpiece. How do I say to one of the richest women in the world; 'The time has come to pay the piper, with the prolonged peter', without her emasculating me?"

Returning to his computer, Dave started typing.

"Frances, I need to raise one point two million dollars immediately. A gang of extortionists have information about one of the Bank's derivative deals that would look very bad for the bank if the press got a hold of it. I was one of the principal executives for our bank in the promotion of the deal. In hindsight, I got the bank into trouble by being too focused on the bottom line. Saying the same thing in another way: I was stupid and you know what Charlie does to people caught being stupid."

He decided that he would not mention the Intimidator Inc. letter. He thought it an inappropriate time to have to explain his relationship with Libby to Frances.

Rereading the email, Dave was satisfied. However, he decided he would review it in the morning before he sent it. Relieved that he had a plan that might save his neck, he called it a night and was soon sound asleep.

The next morning, Dave reread the email and decided to add one final question. As he typed it out, he read it aloud.

"Frances; do you have any ideas how I might get out of the mess I've created?"

Once again, he read the entire email and then he pressed the send button and left for the office.

CHAPTER FIVE

After watching her husband, Charles Van Cleve the 3rd, get into his chauffeur driven Mercedes, Frances Van Cleve returned to the kitchen and sat back down at the breakfast table.

"God, I can't stand Charley going on and on about the fawning cast of characters he has reporting to him at his godforsaken bank." Frances groused to herself. "Why can't he get up in the morning, in a bad mood, and go to the office like everyone else? No, he has to hang around here bugging me with all his ruminations about who he's going to promote and who he's thinking of firing. It's a joke. In twenty years he hasn't fired, or for that matter, demoted a single vice president. He treats them like they were his children. The only one that's really competent is my Dave. But, that has nothing to do with his banking skills. I sure do miss him. I wonder who he's banging over in England? With his endowment, it's probably someone in the Royal family. I hope I'm wrong, for if she decides to keep him handy, she'll probably stash him in the Tower of London. I don't know what I would do if he decided to stay over there."

As she got up from the table and left the kitchen, she saw her image in a mirror. She smiled as she pushed up her breasts and whispered to herself; "Don't worry darlings, I'll find another Dave for you if worse come to worse."

On entering her office, she turned on her computer. She pushed a key and glanced at the list of emails that came up. When she saw she had one from Dave, she immediately opened it.

"What the hell has he done now?" She grumbled, as she read the email. "He's great in the sack; but one point two million? I don't know. Mmm. What the hell, what's money for anyway? He's worth it. But how do I do it? Do I involve Charley, or do I pull it off myself? It's risky one way or the other. If I involve Charley, I put Dave at risk. Charley wouldn't fire him. But, he sure would banish him to the back burner. No, I'm going to have to get it done on my own."

Frances pushed several keys and her account came up on the screen. After studying it carefully, she decided to give Dave eight hundred thousand.

"If I give him the whole amount, he'll not have learned a valuable lesson." She concluded. "Besides, how much more grateful would he be if I gave him the whole amount? No, eight hundred "k" is enough."

"How am I going to deliver the good news?" She pondered. "Why not fly over and deliver the good news to him in his bedroom? God, I like that idea. As soon as Danielle comes in, I'll have her book me on a flight to England tomorrow. Now, how do I break the news to Charley? I'll just tell him that there's a fashion show in London that I've just got to see. He'll eat that story up without me having to bother embellishing it.

Anyway, tomorrow I'm off to Merry Olde England."

The next afternoon, Frances found herself relaxing in the first class section of an American Airlines plane due to arrive in London in the early morning. She chuckled as she reviewed in her mind the events of the last 24 hours and how she had convinced Charley that her trip to London just had to be.

After an uneventful take off, they were soon slipping along the jet stream at their cruising altitude when an attractive man, in his mid forties, started eying her. At first, she ignored him. Then, she decided it might be fun to lead him on. She enjoyed these brief encounters. Nothing ever came of them. But they were important to her because at thirty eight, she had a need to have her beauty frequently confirmed by a new admirer. Pretending to show great interest in the boring book she was reading, she let the hem of her dress slowly climb her slightly parted legs. Her quarry looked longer and became bolder. Finally, he leaned forward and asked; "Your first trip to England?"

Frances, bemused by the success of her strategy, stared at him just long enough to appear to be offended by his effrontery. Then, barely acknowledging his existence, she replied with a drawn out "no".

Then before continuing in a manner that only the intrepid would interrupt, she said: "I've been to the old country many times. One might say I'm truly an anglophile." Then she crushed him by adding: "I assume it's your first visit."

"No. I'm here on business regularly. You see, I'm…." But, before he could finish the sentence, she silenced him with an interjectory dismissal; "That's lovely, but you must get awfully tired of rushing about on commercial airlines. But, please excuse me. I just must finish this book before I meet a dear friend in London."

He could do or say nothing after she dismissed him, except to retreat and plan his next move.

Frances stared into her book but, continued to monitor her admirer's glances. When he seemed to be giving up hope of a conquest, Frances stood up and with her hips swaying erotically she leisurely moved towards the restroom. She could not see what effect this view of her had on her admirer. But, she guessed it would be arousing. She was right, for when she returned, he ask her if he could order her a drink. She accepted graciously, as she did when he proffered a second and a third drink and a fourth over the next two hours. During that time, their conversation had become more and more intimate. Frances looked around the dark cabin and when she saw all her fellow passengers were sound asleep, she allowed him to slide his hand up her thigh and under her dress. But, just as he forced his hand between her legs, the "Fasten Seat Belt" light came on accompanied by the announcement that they were beginning the landing approach.

"You've got to let me know how I can reach you in London." Her admirer pleaded.

"Of course, let me give you a number where you can reach me." Frances whispered and then wrote down an entirely fictitious number and handed it to him.

Her admirer had made a tedious trip enjoyable. Little did he know that Dave O'Connor, who was waiting patiently for Frances in the airport, would profit from his preparatory work.

Dave O'Connor paced the airport waiting room worrying about what would happen to his life if Frances' plane crashed. His eyes never left the "Incoming Flight" display. Suddenly, people were streaming towards him and there was Frances. He spread his arms and she leaped into them.

"Dave," Frances whispered, as she took him by the hand and started walking. "Get me to your hotel room before I rape you. God, I'm turned on. Can we stay in bed the rest of the day? I don't want to share any part of you with anybody."

"Okay, you tasty little morsel, but you've got to calm down. If you don't, you'll have to be content with a stand-in for the beast. Now, that would make all of us very unhappy." Dave cautioned as they climbed into the back seat of a cab.

"Where to mate?" The cabbie inquired.

"The Thistle," and added for Frances sake, "The faster you get there the bigger the tip."

The cabbie took one look at them and started to roll up the security window. But before it closed completely, Frances reached over and clutched Dave's hand. While she stared into Dave's eyes, she pressed his hand up and down her thigh. By the time they reached the hotel, Dave was so anxious to get Frances to his room that he told the cabbie to keep the change from the one hundred pound note he had handed him.

As they pushed their way into Dave's suite, Frances stumbled into his arms when one of the shoes she was trying to remove stubbornly hung up on her little toe. She started to thank him. He silenced her by pressing his lips against her open mouth while he pulled and tugged at her dress. When it fell to the floor, his hands moved up her nearly naked back and unclasp her bra to let her breasts tumble free. Anxiously, he took her by the hand and led her to his bedroom through an opulent three room suite. Momentarily, she was distressed by the way he had chosen to invest in his "creature comfort". She thought; he could have booked at the Hyatt, saved thousands, and still have been pampered.

But, in the bedroom, the blur of the satin upholstered walls quickly faded away as Frances spread her legs and accepted the ecstasy that Dave had been saving for her.

Hours later, Dave's voice woke her from a deep sleep. "Frances, you're a naughty girl. Don't you think it's time we thought of dinner?"

Frances opened her eyes to see Dave sitting on the edge of the bed. "You know what I want for dinner?" He smiled and answered his own question.

"You; you succulent morsel, I want you." He whispered, as his hand massaged her abdomen.

"Dave; stop that. While I get a shower, you pick a place where we can enjoy a nice meal." Frances said, as she rolled out of the far side of the bed.

"Fine Frances; I'm so hungry I could eat you and a boa constrictor." Dave called after her, as she disappeared into the bathroom.

Hours later, as they sat at their table enjoying after dinner drinks, Dave looked at her intently and said:

"God Frances, you're a beautiful woman and I'm the luckiest guy alive. I can't wait to get you back up to the room."

"That's nice Dave. But fun, games, and a roll in the sack must wait. We have something to discuss. Let me see 'the letter". Frances frowned as she read the letter Dave had handed her.

"Do you have any idea how these Russian people found out about us? What do they call themselves?

"Intimidator Inc." Dave answered

"Well," Frances repeated. "Do you have any idea how they found about us?"

"Not really. I've spent a lot of time thinking about it. But, I came up blank."

"Have you noticed anyone lurking around your neighborhood or anyone following you when you're driving to and from work? How about that tart you've been dealing behind my back? What's her name?" Frances asked.

"Elizabeth Foster." Dave sheepishly replied.

"Well, have you ever mentioned my name to her? Now Dave, this is serious business. If you have, I'll forgive you. But I won't, if you lie to me. Do you understand? Now, I'm going to ask one more time. Have you ever mentioned our relationship to Ms. Foster or for that matter, to anyone at all?"

"Never; I know I have my faults." Dave insisted. "But I'm not completely stupid. I love Charley; he's like a father to me. I know he would be destroyed if he knew about our relationship. He's old fashioned and if he knew, it would crush him. No, I'm certain I've never mentioned it to anyone. I won't even ask you, if you have mentioned our relationship to anyone. Because, I know you're a lot smarter than I am. So, we're at square one. How the hell could they have found out about both of my affairs?"

"When I think of it, it's quite simple. You became a potential target when you brokered the derivative deal with the city of Chekhov. All the City Fathers had to do when the deal went bad was to hire Intimidator Inc. and hand them your business card. The Intimidator Inc. people simply hired a local private detective agency. It wouldn't have taken a good detective long to discover what your hobbies were. Don't misunderstand me Dave; I'm not condemning you, I've lifted my skirt more than a few times, myself. Now it appears that this Intimidator Inc. is not a criminal organization. If it were, they would be all over me. But there's no indication that's what's going to happen. Of course, they may have no idea who I am or how wealthy I am. Let's keep it that way if you have any further dealings with them." Frances paused and raising her glass of wine to her lips while staring at Dave. Then Frances continued. "How are you supposed to pay them?"

"I'm to bring a certified check to Mr. Turgenev's room on the last day of the month."

"Well, that gives us almost two weeks to get the money. I won't have any problem getting the 800 K. How are you going to get the 400 K?" Frances asked.

"My only problem will be keeping Samantha in the dark. If she finds out what I've been up to, she'll get a lot more then 400 K from me after she files for divorce."

"If she does leave; will you miss her?" Frances asked.

"Not really. We have very little in common. She's an artist and is into the classics and loves exercising. She's always characterizing my conduct in terms of some ancient Greek geek by the name of Agamemnon. It seems he came home from the Trojan War with a nice young thing named Cassandra. His wife, Clytemnestra, was displeased, so she and her lover, a guy by the name of Aegisthus, dispatched both of them. I'm not sure what Samantha's trying to say with her frequent analogies to these people. It's possible she's dealing some art critic or some jock. I don't know how she could hold any man's interest for any period of time because she has no idea how to put her feminine paraphernalia to any kind of good use."

"You're being cruel. She's a very pleasant woman and I always enjoy her company."

"That's great. But you only see her twice a year. If you had to put up with her nonsense day after day, you would wail a different tale." Dave quipped.

"I'm sorry, Dave. I didn't mean to get off the subject. I'll wire you the 800 "K" in a day or so after I get back to New York. I'll leave the issue of the certified check up to you. You don't anticipate a problem there, do you?"

"It may take a day or so but it should go smoothly." Dave assured her.

"One other thing Dave; what do you plan to do with the Intimidator letter?"

"I planned to burn it. What do you think I should do with it?

"Do you have a lock box? Or maybe I should ask if you have a fire proof lock box?'

"I know what you mean Frances; the letter's a very hot item."

"It could come in handy, Dave. I don't know, and I don't want to know, how you're going to raise the 400 "K". But if something goes wrong, it might be useful to garner sympathy at a divorce trial. If you're certain you can secure it, then it's worth the small risk to retain it."

"You're right, Frances. A good lawyer could probably use its existence to gain sympathy for me from a male judge. I sure wouldn't want a female judge to see it. I'll store it in my safe at home."

"Does Samantha have a key to it?" Frances asked.

"No, it's secured by a combination lock. There's no way she could ever figure out the combination. It will be a perfect hiding spot."

Frances changed the subject by lifting her glass and draining its contents. As she put down her glass, she said to Dave;

"You know we don't have much time. My flight leaves early tomorrow morning." Frances whispered, as she reached under the table and squeezed Dave's thigh and then added.

"Let's get back up to the room; I can't wait to entertain the savage beast and you know how time flies when you're having fun frolicking."

Dave smiled and paid the check. As they walked back to his room, Dave's whole body tingled with anticipation. He wondered if Frances was experiencing the same sensations. She certainly was, as he found out when they entered his room.

The next morning, Dave on his way back from dropping off Frances at Heathrow, smiled to himself when he thought about the "fun" they had shared the night before. After enjoying the memory for a few minutes, his smile turned to a frown when he realized he should call Samantha as soon as he got back to his hotel.

CHAPTER SIX

Samantha had just returned from her run with Desmond. While shedding her jogging gear, the phone began to ring. She answered it when she saw it was Dave.

"Hi Dave," Samantha began mechanically.

"Hi Sam; goods news," He began. "I think I should be able to get back sometime next week. Now if your relationship with your new running buddy is warming up, that might be bad news. In any event, as soon as I can, I'll let you know the date and the flight."

"Fine Dave; I'm sure you must be anxious to get home." Samantha responded again, in a less than enthusiastic tone.

"You sound as though you would like more time with your ancient admirer." Dave quipped sarcastically.

"I don't mean to sound indifferent to what you're saying. But, I'm concerned about why you didn't respond to my Intimidator Inc. question. What's going on, Dave?"

"You artists; you all have such vivid imaginations. Intimidator Inc. is just a small time Russian Collection agency. They're not a big player. Why are you paranoid about them?" Dave barked impatiently.

"Why did you refuse to answer my question about them, when I told you about the television commentator's attitude? That's what made me "paranoid". I think my question was very reasonable." Samantha shot back.

Deciding to soothe Samantha's concerns, Dave responded in his most consoling tone.

"You're absolutely right, Sam. I should have been more sensitive to your anxiety and taken the time to calm your fears. I'm sorry."

Samantha ignored Dave's apology and dismissed him abruptly in a tone which suggested she knew he was lying.

"Well, Dave, if you have nothing better to do, call me in a couple of days; will you?" Annoyed, Samantha thought to herself, "I don't care if he calls or not."

"Okay Sam, I'll call. Talk to you later." Dave countered, impatiently.

As Samantha hung up the phone, she looked out the window to see the mailman putting something in her mailbox. She picked up her jogging suit, put it back on, and strolled out to her mailbox to retrieve the mail. Back in the house, she discarded one piece of junk mail after another until she came to an envelope emblazoned with the name of a company called, 'Sherlock Detective Agency.'

It read:

Dear Ms Samantha O'Connor: You have been randomly selected to be introduced to the services our company provides our customers. We've been in the private detective business for over 60 years. During that time, we've always worked closely with state and local police activities.

Our services include the following:

Civil/Criminal Investigations	Insurance Fraud
Process Services	Records Retrieval
Missing Persons	Video and Phone Surveillance
Child Custody	Debt Collection

Please feel free to call the New York State Department of Commerce & Insurance to check out our qualifications and our reputation.

Mary Bonaro Butler
President of the Sherlock Detective Agency

"Humm, what the hell is behind this?" Samantha exclaimed. "Why would they waste postage sending out advertisements to people picked randomly? The number of people that would ever need a private detective agency has to be less than one percent of the population. I've got to run this by Molly." With that in mind, Samantha picked up the phone and dialed Molly's number.

"Malone here; How may I help you?" Molly answered.

"Hi Molly; it's me, Samantha. Do you have a moment to discuss what I just got in the mail?"

"Sure Sam; what do you have?" Molly asked.

"It's an advertisement sent to me by a company called the Sherlock Detective Agency."

"What do they say?"

"Nothing specific; just general stuff about what they can do and how well they can do it."

"Well Sam; I've heard of them. I've never personally worked a case with them. But plenty of others around here have. Let me get their consensus and I'll get back to you. Probably take a couple hours before I can talk to most of them. Call you back then."

"Thanks Molly. I should be home the rest of day. Talk to you later." Her conversion finished, Samantha hung up the phone, stripped off her damp jogging suit and walked into the kitchen. She poured a cup of coffee and sat down at the kitchen table in her underwear. After thinking about the Collection Agency's letter for a few minutes, she began to mull over her relationship with Desmond. She thought to herself. "I'm getting attached to him. He's old enough to be my father. But I sure don't think of him as my father. He makes me feel good about myself. I so look forward to our morning run. I'm waking up earlier and earlier. He makes me laugh at the world and at my own frailties. It's interesting how easily it is to be truthful, if you disguise it as humor. Dave senses that I really like this guy and in my heart of hearts, I'm not looking forward to Dave's return. I don't want his presence interfering with the relationship that's growing between Desmond and me.

"Ouch; that's hot." Samantha exclaimed, for she had closed her legs around the hot coffee cup she had been holding between her thighs.

"God, what made me do that?" She cried out, smiling, as she raised the cup to her lips. After draining its contents, she rose from the table and headed for the shower. Several hours later, Molly called back.

"Sam, I've got the story on the Sherlock Agency. They're reputable. The guys here have nothing but good things to say about them. My captain mentioned a peculiarity in their operating procedure. When an investigation reveals a husband to be a philanderer, they always send an advertisement brochure to his home address."

"That doesn't make any sense. Why would they do that, Molly?"

"The Sherlock Agency's president is a woman. Apparently, it's her subtle way of informing the person, 'who's always the last to know', that she may have a problem."

"God, that's upsetting. What receiving this brochure means, is that someone hired Sherlock to investigate Dave's habits and found that his wife should be told about them. Like I said; I'm upset. But, I'm not surprised. Who hired the Sherlock Agency and why would someone care who Dave O'Connor was dealing?"

"Well Sam, somebody cared and it sure looks like someone wanted the information so they could extort money from your Dave. Now, who do you think that might be?"

"Intimidator Inc." Samantha shouted out, almost gleefully.

"And there's more; the Sherlock Agency informed our department that they had a request to investigate your Dave. Their customer was a private citizen. But, you can be certain they were working for

Intimidator Inc. As you've already guessed, they found Dave has been involved with a woman. Her name is Frances Van Cleve. Do you know her?"

"I'll say, I know, her! She's the wife of the CEO of the bank Dave works for. God, how could he be so stupid? If Charley ever found out about the love birds, Dave would be out of a job and she would be out on the street."

"I assume Charley is the lady's husband and the CEO?"

"Yes. What a mess; this is so awful I can't believe it's happening to me. Molly, I've got to hang up. I can hardly get my breath. I think I'm having some kind of panic attack. I'm going outside and walk around the block. Maybe that will help. I'll get back to you as soon as I can."

"Sam, give me a couple of minutes, I'll be right there. If you go outside, stay close to your house. Now, Sam, please listen carefully to me. If you're having a serious attack, you're going to start sweating and your heart will begin to pound. You'll feel like you're choking and that you're going to die. But remember, and this is very important, the attack will last less than ten minutes. I'll be there shortly, I'm on my way."

"No Molly; I'll be okay, I'm going outside, right now. I'm sorry….." Suddenly, Samantha stopped talking for she realized Molly had hung up. She put down her phone and raced to the front door and stepped out into the sunshine. Immediately, the panic started to leave her. When it was almost gone, she started to sob uncontrollably.

"My world's falling apart. Fuck! Do I divorce him or do I live with his frailties? I can accept his indifference. But, I dread going through a divorce. I can't deal with lawyers. But, what I really can't deal with is paying them so much for doing so little. I think I'll just take the attitude that if he can; I can. Last fall, the stud from the carpet store looked like he wanted to lay me more then he did the carpet. Maybe I should get the bed room carpeted before Dave gets back? I'll bet a connection, with that Adonis, would leave me smiling for a week."

Samantha's recall of the carpet kid's physique curbed her tears and provoked her tongue to moisten her lips. As she did, she looked up to see Debbie Logan lumbering towards her.

"Oh God no, I can't get away. She's seen me. Damn; I'm trapped." Samantha immediately began to dab her eyes in a vain attempt to remove any telltale sign of tears.

"Hi Samantha;" Debbie beamed. "It's been so long. Whatever have you and Dave been doing?"

"Hi Debbie; what's happening with you and Frank?" Samantha asked in a perfunctory voice. Then, she thought to herself, "I hope you're going to be brief."

But Debbie was never brief. She insisted on going on and on about every little detail of her humdrum existence. Finally, she stopped and looked intently into Samantha's face.

"Sam!" She exclaimed; "you've been crying. What's the matter?" She asked, with genuine interest.

"It's just allergies. I'm fine." Samantha fibbed.

"Well, if it's not allergies and you need to talk to someone, I can control my compulsive talking when someone really needs a listener."

Samantha was struck and surprised by Debbie's sensitivity which she had never imagined Debbie possessed. "Thank you, Deb. That's very sweet of you. Someday, let's just do that."

"I hope so Samantha. Right now I have to run. The kids will be home shortly and Frank likes to eat as soon as he walks in the door. So, I've got to run." Without waiting for a response, Debbie embraced Samantha and hurried off leaving Samantha to ponder a side of Debbie she had never suspected existed. As she stood there watching Debbie disappear around the block, a car rolled to a stop beside her.

"Hi Sam;" The voice of Molly Malone called out from the car. "I see you beat the demon. Would you like a ride home?"

CHAPTER SEVEN

Samantha had retired early. Exhausted by the events of the day, she had fallen asleep almost immediately. But, she had not remained so. Suddenly, wide awake, she rolled over and stared at the bedside clock.

"Ah, I can't believe it. I've only slept two hours and I know damn well I won't be able to get back to sleep. Damn it! That goddamn Dave. What the hell do these crazy women see in him? He's overweight, he's balding, and unless he's talking about banking, he talks like a teenager. When he discusses banking, all he does is brag about how many investors he screwed by convincing them to buy worthless derivatives. Somehow, his wild dealings with powerful people around the world excite his female admirers. Why would Frances Van Cleve even look at him, let alone leap into the sack with him? She's got to be turned on by the danger of their liaison. Charley is such a good person; but Frances doesn't care. You know, I'm making an assumption there. Maybe Charley ignores her or belittles her. Maybe Charley has a harem. He sure enough could afford one. Forget Frances; why does Dave wander? I'm still an attractive woman and I work very hard to keep my figure for him. Am I kidding myself? Why do I work like hell to keep my figure while the typical woman, in this community, eats with both hooves and looks like Debbie? Simply, it's because trim ladies get lots and lots of admiring looks from men. I wonder if my need for the attention of intelligent men offends Dave? Does my conduct, although innocent, undermine his satisfaction with our marriage? Does he need the intimacy of other women to relieve his anxiety over my lukewarm commitment to our relationship?

I hate myself for letting Dave humiliate me. But, did I encourage his conduct so I could become what I desired to be? Did I succumb to his cajoling and conniving words so I could flaunt the creature comforts he has provided? Certainly I've played a role in creating the mess which is now our marriage. Unlike him, though, I've not strayed physically. But, the more I think about us, the less innocent I feel. I know, no matter how guilty I am; I'm convinced he is by far the more culpable. Now, I'm not really sure whether I despise him more than I despise myself. Dave has unwittingly freed me and I'm going to enjoy it. He's still my meal ticket. If he decided to leave, the bus ticket out of town would cost him a fortune. But right now, he has to be punished. How can I do that? I could leap into the sack with a butcher, a baker or a candlestick maker or with all three of them. But that's not me. I'm not going to let just any guy sweet talk me out of my underwear. He's going to have to be special because I can afford to be particular. I didn't keep this chassis fit to let just anyone's hands explore it. He's going to have to be special, and it's going to be fun, really fun, when he discovers what I can do to delight him. All this is pleasing to think about but, how rehashing it over and over again, going to help me deal with Dave?

Sometimes, to punish someone, you might have to use a special skill. If you're big and strong, you can simply beat the hell out of them. If you look like Cleopatra, you can deny them your presence. If you have a tongue like a serpent, you can spit poison into their ears. But, what special skill do I have? Hell, I'm an artist. Didn't Oscar Wilde write something about a bizarre portrait that showed the subject aging while the flesh and blood person remained young and virile? That's it. I'll do a portrait of what I think Dave will look like if he ever gets to be an old man. Ah! Perfect; and I might as well get started now. Sleep is out of the question." Samantha cried; as she rolled out of the bed and slid into a smock while entering her studio. After setting up a new canvas, she began to paint. Hours passed. Slowly, the image of an old man began to emerge from the canvas. He was bald, wrinkled and pathetic. The head rested precariously on the shoulders. The eyes were lifeless. Sadness clouded the face.

Almost finished, she stopped and stared at the painting. It was Dave at eighty; his spirit withered and his power to hurt her destroyed forever. She was strangely elated and then she realized that painting Dave, as he someday would be, had freed her from him. She put down her brush and looked approvingly at the painting. It was the best work she had ever done. It was her masterpiece. She titled it "Released" and she thought; "It's amazing what the intellect can create when it's serving a passion."

As she turned from the painting, her eye caught the clock. "It's five thirty. Desmond will be here in 30 minutes. I've got to move." She cried. Before leaving her studio, she stared at the portrait and purred; "Dave will be upset; particularly after I add a few more wrinkles. Anyway Dave," she said addressing the portrait. "I have got to run. But you can be certain, I'll be back."

She put down her brush and rushed upstairs and donned her jogging gear. By the time she returned, Desmond was lightly tapping on her front door.

"Good morning Des. Have you been waiting long?" She said, as she opened the door.

"I've just arrived. How're you doing this morning?" he inquired. Samantha looked at Desmond and thought to herself, "I wonder if there's any truth to the old story about old guys being patient lovers?"

"I'm fine Des. All set to go. Shall we?"

They had only been running a few minutes when Desmond broke the silence. "Sam, at the moment the police suspect that I took the knife or that it didn't exist. Now, I don't know how sophisticated the gear was that the police used in their search for the knife. But, I suspect it was 'state of the art'. I know you're telling the truth and

I know I am. So, where does that leave us? A third person has to be involved. How far did you run before Wilber caught up with you?"

"I'm really not sure. I would guess forty to sixty feet. But, it could have been further. As I said, I'm just not sure; your point?" Samantha asked.

"All the time I had Wilber held down, we had very little conversation. I had warned him what would happen if he opened his mouth. My point is this. Someone could have come by and not heard us, pickup the knife and simply took it home with them."

"Improbable Des, but I concede it could have happened that way. If it did, what can we do?" Samantha asked

"The first thing we do is locate a store that sells scuba gear. When I get home, I'll try to find one on the internet. If I do, and you agree, I'll come over this afternoon and we'll drive there. We'll look at all their knives and if they have one that looks anything like Wilber's, we'll buy it. Then, we'll take it to Molly and have her get a picture of it printed on the front page of our local newspaper with an explanation of why the police want the knife. If the person who found it reads newspapers, we'll have our knife."

"I don't know Des; but at least it's a possibility. You know, now that you mention it, I remember reading about how a serial murderer was caught when he left the murder knife at the scene of his last murder. The knife had one of its handle's retaining rivets missing. A relative of the murderer recognized the knife from the picture, and reported the guy to the local police. They arrested him, but not before he had murdered three or four more people." Samantha rued.

"Okay; then do we agree?" Desmond asked.

"Yes, it's a long shot. But, the odds of finding the 'knife' buried in a deep hole are even bleaker. How about one o'clock?" Samantha asked, as they approach her house.

"Okay; I'll be here at one." Desmond agreed and they parted.

Once inside, Samantha decided that she would dress up for the trip to the store. "I'm wondering; can I get a sixty year old guy to leer at me if I package myself right? I'm going to go with my black silk skirt and my low cut white lace blouse. I'll modestly cover the view with that conspicuous black jacket that I bought in New York last fall. All-in-all, it should get me a few furtive glances."

Having decided on her wardrobe, Samantha called Molly and brought her up to date on the plan. To Samantha's surprise, Molly liked the idea and felt certain she could get the local newspaper to co-operate if they located a duplicate of the knife. When Samantha told her they planned to visit the scuba store that afternoon, Molly requested they bring her any knife they might find.

After their phone conversation ended, Samantha spent the rest of the morning preparing herself for the scuba store venture as she, herself, called it. Precisely at one P.M., Desmond rapped on her front door.

"Come in Desmond." Samantha said, as she opened the door.

"Hi, I guess I'm not too early since I see you're all ready to go." He said but, showed no trace of appreciation for all work she had done to make herself easy on his eyes. Her disappointment vanished when he added; "Stunning Samantha; you look very nice." He said politely but his scanning eyes said it a lot more emphatically. Samantha was pleased and smiled to herself, as she and Desmond drove off in his car.

"The store they call The Scuba Dive is located downtown." Desmond began. "I expect we can get there within twenty minutes or so. You know, Sam, we've been jogging together for over a week now and I still don't know a great deal about you. Where are you from and how long have you and your husband lived here?" Desmond asked politely.

"We moved here almost ten years ago when Charlie promoted Dave to a vice president position at the home office of his Honrado Bank here in New York. Dave had been the manager of a small bank in Clarkston, Michigan and had been phenomenally successful or phenomenally lucky in making his Clarkston Honrado bank phenomenally profitable."

"I assume Charlie is the CEO of Honrado Bank?" Desmond queried.

"Yes Charlie is Charles Morgan Van Cleve the Third and despite his fancy moniker is a very down to earth and lovable man.

If he has a weakness, it's that he's too trusting of his vice presidents. That can lead to serious problems if one or more of them sell toxic mortgages to powerful and unforgiving people."

"The banking business is perilous these days. You skate on thin ice when you hoodwink powerful people." Desmond asserted and then asked. "Where did you meet your husband?"

"We took a of couple classes together at Michigan State. Dave did not work hard on courses like business ethics. But I did, so I tutored him. After we graduated, we dated for several months and then we married and the rest was typical until Dave got promoted. When we arrived here, I enrolled in an Art School in New York City. I had always loved to draw and paint. But after attending school, my interest really grew. In fact, my agent is now in the process of arranging for a show of my paintings. Of course, now, that will have to wait until this mess is resolved."

"Do you have children?" Desmond asked. "No, we don't." Samantha responded; almost apologetically. "Dave has always resisted the idea of a family." After answering Desmond's question, she fell silent and stared out the window for an extended period of time. Desmond picked up on her sensitivity of the subject and let the conversation lag. After a few minutes, Samantha broke the silence. "Do you have a family, Des?" Samantha asked.

"Yes, I have a daughter who lives in California and a son who works on the North Slope in Alaska. My daughter's married to a physicist who teaches at Cal Tech. They have two small daughters. My son has never married and if he stays in Alaska, he probably never will. The only women who live on the North Slope are either married or frozen stiff or both." Desmond paused and fell silent which prompted Samantha to comment.

"And where's your wife Desmond?"

"Dianne is Dianne; we were together for 25 years. But I'm a geologist and sometimes geologists spend months in the field. She got lonely and now she's married to a guy who's a 'shooter' at Chevron in San Ramon, California, where they live. We're on good terms and we communicate regularly." Just as Dave finished speaking, they pulled up in front of 'The Scuba Dive'.

Despite its name, its interior was well lit and its inventory well presented. Once inside, they were greeted by a young athletic looking man who encouraged their search, once they had explained their purpose. It did not take long before Samantha cried out that she had found, what she exclaimed, was an exact duplicate of the knife Coirpeach had used to assault her. After intently staring at the knife, for a long moment, she cried out; "Yes, I'm certain. It's the knife. Yes, it's definitely the knife!"

Desmond purchased the knife and they were shortly on their way to see Molly, at the police station. Once there, it did not take Samantha long to convince Molly they had an identical copy of the missing knife. Molly then agreed that she would ask the local newspaper to publish a picture of the knife. As they left the police station, Molly requested and received from Samantha, the name and address of 'The Scuba Dive'.

On the way home, in the car, Samantha wondered out loud why Molly wanted the store's address.

"She probably wants to see if they have a record of whom they might have sold that type of knife to in the past." Desmond casually suggested.

Desmond's comment started Samantha wondering whose name might be on such a list. The more she thought about it; the more she worried. Then she asked herself; "Could Dave have been that stupid? If he's involved, what the hell was his motive? I've got to get back into that strong box. Maybe I missed something."

Lost in thought she didn't realize that Desmond had brought the car to a stop in her own driveway.

"Thanks Desmond. I would invite you in for coffee but my inquisitive neighbors are watching." She quipped as she got out of the car. "I'll see you in the morning." She added, as she pushed the car door closed.

Desmond simply nodded his agreement and drove off preoccupied with his own thoughts.

CHAPTER EIGHT

Samantha walked up to her front door, turned, and waved good bye to Desmond's departing car, as she entered her home. Once inside, after closing the door, she mumbled quietly to herself.

"He's a nice human being. I'm really getting fond of him." She smiled and then after a moment, lost in thought, she continued. "But right now, I've got to slip out of these designer clothes and go through the safe, again. But before I do that; I'm going to have dinner."

An hour later, as Samantha was putting her dinner dishes away, Molly called.

"Hi Sam; I'm sorry, but I've got some disturbing news." After an awkward pause Molly continued. "A person using a Visa card, issued to one David O'Connor, purchased the same type of knife from The Scuba Dive you showed me this afternoon." Again Molly paused and when there was only silence, she continued. "If you have your credit card handy, I'll read you off the number of the card the person used."

Samantha put Molly on hold and retrieved her credit card. Back on the phone, Samantha asked Molly if she was ready to compare the numbers. Without hesitating Molly read Samantha the number of the card used to buy the knife. Samantha confirmed that the numbers matched; Molly added: "Sam I don't really understand what's happening here. Someone used your Visa card to buy the knife that Elmer used to assault you. Do you have any idea why anyone would want you to be raped by some scumbag?"

"Molly, it makes no sense to me. But I can say this, no matter what the evidence suggests, there's just no way Dave would have set me up to be raped. I know it sounds contradictory, but I want to be absolutely certain about Dave, so I'm going back into the safe and fine comb every document in there. I probably won't be able to get back to you this afternoon. But, if I find anything, I'll call you first thing in the morning."

"Sam, I know this whole mess has got to be getting to you. But if your Dave's involved, we've got to start thinking of protection for you. If he hired Coirpeach, and I'm not saying he did. But, if he did hire him, he's dangerous- very dangerous." Molly cautioned. When Samantha didn't respond to Molly's warning, Molly continued; "Sam, are you still there?"

"I'm sorry, Molly. It just seems that every other day my world comes crashing down around me. I just can't believe Dave would subject me to such terrifying experience. He's not the most ethical money changer in the temple. But he's not a monster. If he did this, what on earth could have compelled him to do such a thing to any women, let alone his wife? I just can't accept that he's involved. I keep praying some explanation will surface that will exonerate him. But, I'm beginning to feel hopeless. I'll let you know if I find anything in the safe."

"Okay, if you do, call me back immediately. Something has come up here. I expect I'll be here for at least another hour."

Samantha agreed, hung up the phone, and walked into Dave's office. She pulled a chair over to the safe, sat down, and careful dialed in the lock's combination. Then, with a quick pull, she snapped opened the lock. She took everything out of the box and placed all the papers on Dave's table. Carefully, she leafed through each document. Nothing alerted her until she reached a brochure titled 'Visit Scotland the Brave'. After briefly scanning the brochure, she realized it was a typical advertisement urging wealthy people to come and visit Loch Leven Castle where Mary Queen of Scots had been a prisoner. Enclosed in the brochure, along with a receipt, was a letter congratulating a Mr. and Mrs. David O'Connor for having the good taste to have spent a week at the Castle. Samantha looked at the date of the stay and realized that there was more than one Mrs. "David O'Connor". She was not pleased. But, when she saw that the "pop in" at the Castle had cost three thousand pounds, she became infuriated. "God damn his philandering ass." As Samantha reread the brochure, she rose from the chair and as she did, she caught her own reflection in the mirror on the wall. The image of the angry woman she saw immediately brought to her mind the Bible's warning; 'Hell hath no fury, like a woman scorned'. Then recalling Molly's suggestion of protection for her, she screamed out: "God damn him; when I get my hands on that son of bitch, he'll be the one that needs police protection."

She rushed around the office flailing the letter from Scotland before collapsing into Dave's plush office chair. With her face buried in her hands and her anger spent, she moaned.

"I've got to accept it. I can't live with him any longer. I've got to think. What he's been doing is so stupid that maybe the guilt of selling all those useless derivatives to innocent people has destroyed his good judgment. Oh stop Samantha! You know damn well that he's hood winked you for years. All you've ever done is to look the other way because he gave you all the conspicuous wealth that your ego needed. It was damn careless of him to leave this brochure in his safe. But then, who would have thought a mere housewife could figure out the combination of his precious lock? Maybe he wants to be caught. Maybe it's a cry for help? Maybe he needs me? Then again maybe, I need my head read?" Samantha paused, took a deep breath, picked up the phone, and dialed Molly's number.

Reading her caller I.D., Molly answered her phone.

"Hi Sam; what have you got?"

Samantha explained what she had found in the safe and emphasized that she found nothing that could tie him to the attack on her.

"Well Samantha, I'm very happy for you." Not being able to say anything consoling to Samantha concerning her personal problems with Dave, Molly abruptly changed the subject.

"Now, if we can locate the knife that Coirpeach used to attack you, it will add credence to your version of what happened in the woods and you can stop worrying about that issue."

Molly paused to allow Samantha time to consider her response. When she heard nothing after waiting for what she thought was an appropriate length of time, Molly finally asked; "Are you there Sam?"

"Oh God; I'm here. But oh how I wish I where anywhere else. How could that bastard go off to Scotland with some bimbo and frolic with her for a week? How could he do that to me? If he were here, I would scratch his eyes out." Samantha sobbed and began to whimper. "How could he do that? How could he?" Samantha wailed and then fell silent. Molly said nothing for she expected Samantha's anger would soon give way to anguish. When it did, she would try to comfort her.

"What can I do, Molly?" Samantha pleaded. "He's been my whole life for over twenty years. Now I have to start all over again. I'm frightened. I'm totally dependent on him. I'm almost 50 years old and I'm alone. I know; the good ones are gone. I can see myself being mauled in the back seat of some tattooed guy's car who thinks he owns me because he bought me French fries and a hamburger. I have no idea what our financial situation is. For him to do what he did, we have to be on the road to the poor house. Maybe I'll have to get a job cleaning other people's houses. All these years the thought of growing old with him didn't particularly thrill me. But, I was comfortable with the long and short of it. Can I choke on my pride and forgive him? God, I don't see how I can live in the same house with him, let alone lie in the same bed. I know I can't make a decision when my mind's preoccupied with what's going on in my stomach. But, what on earth could have driven him to behave in such a blatant fashion? I can't forgive or condone what he has done. But I'm going to listen to what he has to say for himself. I'm going to sleep on the whole mess, not just tonight, but for many nights, before I make a final decision. Molly, I don't want to burden you anymore than I have today. I'm going to let you go and I'm going to go sit in front of the television and drink a bottle of wine. Thank you Molly; for listening to me. I'm sorry for burdening you. Please forgive me."

"Are you all right Sam? Would it help, if I came over and listened?"

"No Molly. It's my problem and I'm going to solve it. But right now I'm on my way to get that bottle of wine. Good night Molly and thanks for being my friend."

After Samantha hung up the phone, she recalled that Molly had not said anything about the date the knife was purchased. Samantha mumbled out loud: "I can check the date out on-line. If the knife purchase was charged against our Visa account, the debit will be listed." She turned on the computer. With a few clicks, she accessed their account statement. Sure enough, the amount and date of The Scuba Dive debit was listed. Right below it was a debit charge on the same day by a restaurant in Farmington, Michigan. Then it hit her. Dave had flown to Detroit, Michigan, on the day before, to attend the funeral of a boyhood friend. Scanning up the debit listings, she found a debit for an airline ticket to Detroit and there below it was one for a Farmington Hills hotel room. Dave had been out of town the day the knife had been purchased.

"I just knew he wasn't a monster. I'm sure not pleased with Dave, but at least I'm no longer afraid of him. It had to be that scumbag Coirpeach who purchased the knife. But how did he get our Visa Card number? It's mind boggling. I'm going to call Molly first thing in the morning. Maybe she'll come up with some explanation. I'm sure she'll be pleased with what I've found. Maybe she'll even suggest that I would be good lady cop. Anyway, I'm off to bed and the hell with the bottle of wine."

CHAPTER NINE

Samantha had just returned from jogging with Desmond. It had been an interesting run. Their conversation had dealt with issues that men and women usually do not discuss together. She did most of the talking, but Desmond listened attentively to what she had to say. To her own surprise, she had been candid discussing her sexual activity while attending college. She sensed that Desmond listened with more than casual interest to what she had to say. She realized that her growing dissatisfaction with her marriage had created the desire to discuss the subject with Desmond. She wondered if her fondness for him was responsible for her broaching such a sensitive subject. She looked into the bathroom mirror and smiled at herself. She knew she had purposely opened up a window of opportunity for Desmond, if he were interested. She realized it would not be long before she knew if she had kindled a fire in her friend.

Her musing was abruptly interrupted by a ringing telephone, which she answered when she saw it was Molly.

"Good morning, Molly. What's up?"

"Good news, very good news; we have your knife. Your friend, Desmond, was right; a jogger found it. He saw the picture of the knife in last night's paper and brought the knife to me first thing this morning. Unfortunately, his prints are all over it. Its established existence strongly supports your version of what happened. He found it just about where you thought it might be."

"Molly, I can't...... or should I say I can't even begin to tell you how relieved I am. But, listen to this; I also have very good news."

Samantha announced proudly and went on to explain how she had discovered that Dave had been in Michigan the day the knife had been purchased at Scuba Dive.

"Great Sam. That's great news. You must be ecstatic. I'm really very happy for you. Does a possibility exist now that the two of you might work things out?"

"I don't know about that. He's still a philandering bastard and I know it's unlikely he'll ever change his ways. I've got to decide if I can help him overcome his demons or if I am I just putting off the inevitable. At least, now I have time to carefully consider my options."

Molly waited for Samantha to continue. But when she fell silent, Molly changed the subject.

"Since Dave didn't purchase the knife. Whoever did must have had your Visa Card number. Sure, Dave could have given it to anybody. But why would your husband risk implicating himself? The more important question is; why would Wilber Coirpeach or anyone else even bother to purchase the knife with your Visa Card? Wilber certainly didn't have the resources to have obtained its number on his own. So, what does this all add up to? It means that whoever arranged to purchase the knife with your card's number has considerable resources and had the smarts to make it look like Dave orchestrated the assault on you. The culpable party has to be Intimidator Inc. They must have arranged what happened to you to put more pressure on Dave, in case he didn't knuckle under to their threat to expose his various liaisons. Then again, Intimidator Inc. may want to cite what you experienced as a warning to other banking executives. The message being; capitulate to our financial demands or your wife might have to endure a very unpleasant experience."

"Why wouldn't anyone," Samantha asked, "who was being pressured to cough up money to Intimidator, Inc. just go to the police and ask for protection?"

"If you had sold a bunch of worthless mortgage derivatives to innocent people by lying to them, would you be anxious to get the police involved?" Molly replied. "What's the definition of thievery? More importantly what's the penalty for stealing millions of dollars from innocent people? What's the penalty for creating havoc in the world's financial system?"

"Well Molly, we've all heard the catchy phrase; "too big to fail". A more fitting phrase might be, "too big to jail". But, in all fairness, the pressure on the people who call the shots in the financial system must be enormous. If the profits are not there, the bank's board of directors leans on their CEO and he leans on his various vice presidents who then lean on their people. If the bottom line turns red, the board will get someone, in a hurry, to turn it back to black.

If one bank starts to make a lot of money using some new financial hocus-pocus, it won't be long before many other banks adopt the same strategy. That's what happened with derivatives. Most bankers were too busy using them to realize how dangerous their use could be. Oh, I'm sure plenty of banking people spoke out against their use. But, when the money's rolling in, it's very easy to ignore any warning.

In Berkshire's 2002 annual report Warren Buffett said: "In our view, however, derivatives are financial weapons of mass destruction, carrying dangers that, while now latent, are potentially lethal." What I find unconscionable is that our political leaders completely ignored a dire warning from the world's most successful investor."

"Sam, how come you know so much about financial goings on?" Molly asked.

"It was my minor at MSU. And from what I've seen lately, I'm sure glad it wasn't my major. But now, let's discuss a very pressing event. Dave arrives back tomorrow afternoon. Any suggestions on how I should handle his return?" Samantha asked.

"I expect you have given his return a lot of thought. Have you reached any conclusions of your own?" Molly asked.

"I'm going to lay it all out for him. How he responds to what I have to say will determine what I finally do. Are you going to have to talk to him?" Samantha asked.

"Not immediately. I'm going to have to get the F.B.I. involved first."

"Why involve the F.B.I.?" Samantha asked.

"Well, it appears that Intimidator Inc. is running an international extortion operation. Since their crime is international, the F.B.I. must be involved in any attempt to prosecute them. I think we both know that your husband will be, at best, a reluctant witness. Without his cooperation, the likelihood of a trial, let alone a conviction, is extremely unlikely. The F.B.I. is probably up to their derriere's investigating various banking frauds and will probably conclude that Dave got his just dessert from Intimidator Inc. Of course, I could never officially say that about the "august" F.B.I., so don't quote me." Molly said, with a smile on her face, suggesting some inter agency conflict might exist. After nodding her agreement with Molly, Samantha then asked;

"Do you think the District Attorney will put Wilber Coirpeach on trial?"

"I know you're not going to be happy. But the D.A. will probably plea bargain the case. I suspect Wilber will go along with a year in custody."

"I know it's not your fault. But it's incredible to me, that a guy can do what he did and walk out a free man in a year or two."

"I understand how you feel Sam. But, that's justice in the U. S. of A. today."

"Well Molly, I'll say one thing positive about the justice system, and that is; I'm glad you're part of it and I want to thank you for every thing you've done. I'm going to let you go now so I can think about what I'm going to say to Dashing Dave when he walks into the house tomorrow afternoon. I'll talk to you later Molly."

"Okay, Sam."

CHAPTER TEN

Dave O'Connor walked into the lobby of the Calvendish Hotel and approached the clerk standing behind the desk.

"Would you please announce my arrival to Mr. Ivan Turgenov in room 1122?"

"May I have your name sir?" The clerk replied. When Dave told him his name, the clerk picked up the phone and dialed room 1122.

"Mr. Turgenov, a Mister David O'Connor is here to see you. Shall I send him up?" The clerk asked.

Dave heard a muffled response and then the clerk said:

"Mr. Turgenov would be pleased to see you Mr. O'Connor. You'll find the elevators to the eleventh floor on your right, sir."

Dave arrived at the elevator just as its doors opened. He waited patiently as a number of people rushed out. Finally empty, he and a couple entered the elevator. The man pushed the button for the twelfth floor. When he stepped back, Dave move forward and pushed the button for the eleventh floor. When Dave backed away from the elevator's control panel, he turned to the couple and said good evening.

The man muttered something in a foreign language that Dave guessed might be Russian. The woman only smiled.

Dave thought to himself, "Is this hotel full of Russians?"

A few moments passed. The elevator doors opened and Dave walked out onto the eleventh floor. Arriving at room 1122, he noticed a burly man sitting on a chair, in an alcove opposite the door, reading a newspaper. The man nodded as Dave knocked on the door. In a moment the door opened and Dave was welcomed into the room by Mr. Turgenov.

"Thank you for coming, Mr. O'Connor." Ivan Turgenov began. "You are more than prompt Mr. O'Connor. I expect that's a characteristic common to the people in your profession."

"Indeed it is, Mr.Turgenov. I have a certified check for you. It is made out for the sum of one point two million dollars. You may deposit it as soon as tomorrow morning."

Dave said, as he handed Mr. Turgenov the check.

"Thank you, Mr. O'Connor. I have a receipt in that amount for you. As you know, we are a charitable organization and your contribution, I think, is probably tax deductible. However, you'll have to confirm that with your Internal Revenue Service."

"I confess that possibility had never occurred to me, Mr.Turgenov. It certainly is something I'll look into."

"You're most welcome, Mr. O'Connor. But now I must confess that I have pressing business that I must attend to. Unless you have something still to discuss, you'll have to excuse me."

"Certainly, Mr.Turgenov; I understand and I must say it has been a pleasure doing business with you." Dave said, as he reached out and shook Mr.Turgenov's extended hand. Mr. Turgenov then escorted Dave to the door. Dave said good night and walked out the door.

On the way down in the elevator, Dave mused to himself. "Hell, if I handle this tax deductible thing right, I might even be able to turn a profit on the whole deal. Of course, that would mean screwing Frances by claiming the whole contribution. What the hell, I've screwed her before. But, if she ever found out what I had done, she would be the one doing the screwing."

Dave was still mulling over the income tax deduction idea when he emerged from the Calvendish. After looking in vain for a cab, he decided to walk back to the Thistle. Almost there, his thoughts turn to Libby Foster.

"God, I wouldn't mind slipping it to Libby. I wonder what she's doing tonight. A nice roll in the sack with her would be a fitting end for the agony of the last three weeks.

The Honcho certainly has created a very imperfect world which would be impossible to tolerate if it weren't for the solace a good sack session bestows on a man and a woman. No wonder the celibates in this world are all strange and unpredictable.

It's getting late and I've got to catch that damn early flight back to New York. Down beast, it's too late to enjoy Libby tonight. You have to be hungry when we arrive home or you won't be able to service the lady with the broom."

On arriving back at the Thistle, Dave scanned the lobby. When nothing of interest caught his eye, he accepted that the day was over and reluctantly retreated to his room.

CHAPTER ELEVEN

Samantha had been waiting all afternoon and finally Dave's car appeared in the driveway. She opened the front door and greeted him coolly as he lugged a heavy suitcase up the steps of the front porch. Undeterred by her aloofness, he tried to kiss her on the lips. But, his kiss landed on a cold ear.

"What's the matter? I know; your broom broke. That's it, isn't it?" He quipped.

"We've got something to discuss." Samantha hissed.

"Samantha, I'm still lugging my suitcase and you're starting a goddamn argument. If you want one, shut the damn door and I'll verbally choke you. Now, what the hell's the matter with you?" Dave barked, as he threw his heavy suitcase into the hall closet.

"Sit down!" She screamed.

"Sit down yourself, you silly bitch." He said as he sat down.

"I'll tell you; what's the matter. Frances Van Cleve and Elizabeth Foster is what the matter is. You know all about them. Or should I say? You know what's under their clothes. How stupid of you to bed down your boss's wife. Every woman, whose husband is somebody in the company, knows that Frances Van Cleve has a firestorm in her panties. Don't you cowboys talk about you're conquests? And the other tart makes her bread by lying flat on her back in a perfumed water bed. You idiot, you could have brought anything home from a toss in the sack with her. God, you're stupid!"

All Dave could do was stare at Samantha with his mouth wide open while his brain frantically searched for any kind of fitting response to his wife's hysterical accusations. His first thought was to deny everything. But, he realized she had the goods on him. Then, he thought he would plead for mercy. But, he knew it was too early to beg for forgiveness. Finally, in desperation, he accused her of having oral sex with the kid that installed the carpet.

Samantha dismissed his accusation with such acrimony that he wished he had not dreamt up the charge. Finally, he just sat there like a felon, restrained in a pillory, while his wife verbally shredded his self esteem with her razor sharp tongue.

Red eyed and red faced Samantha ran from the room and disappeared up the stairs leaving Dave sitting there, befuddled by his lack of options.

"Strange, I actually feel relieved. Secretly, I must have wanted her to know I could please other women. I don't know if that's it or not. But, I do know I'm damn tired of the life we live. I know it's not her fault. But, our boat is sinking and I don't want to sink with it. I know I have the appetite of a teenager and the good sense of a moron. I just can't fight off these women who are as dissatisfied with their lives as I am with mine. Hell, when I hold one of them in my arms, I'm young again. It's not Sam's fault. It's the way I'm made. I really don't want to hurt her. But, I don't want to die of boredom either.

How the Hell am I going to get out of this mess? If only that cluck she runs with would deal her, we could both forgive one another. Now that she's beyond my reach, the thought of 'makeup sex' with her is absolutely titillating. Down beast, both of us know it's not going to happen.

Maybe I can sweet talk her. I suspect she's too thrifty to pay some low life lawyer to take me to the cleaners. I've got to think. How the hell do I get out of this mess? Best that I be humble and plead for forgiveness. I can do that. I'll start by taking out the garbage. There should be some around here.

What the hell is that noise? God, she's wailing like a banshee. Okay, I'll go upstairs and launch my strategy."

Dave quietly climbed the stairs, opened the door to their bedroom, and peered into the darkened room. Samantha lay on the bed sobbing uncontrollably. Dave entered the bedroom, pulled a chair over to the bed, and sat down in it. Samantha ignored his presence. After a few minutes, Dave reached over and gently touched her hand. Instantly, Samantha bolted from the bed and raced into the bathroom and slammed the door behind her. Dave made no attempt to stop her. Realizing it would be a while before she returned he simply crawled into the bed and quickly feel asleep.

Several hours later, Dave awoke with the light from the bedside lamp shining into his eyes and Samantha screaming for him to get out of the bed. Dave turned over and went back to sleep. Samantha reached over and started pulling on his shirt in an attempt to get him out of the bed.

"What the hell's the matter with you, you silly bitch? I'm too tired for sex now. Leave me alone." He quipped.

Samantha barely managed to suppress the urge to laugh out loud at his humor. Exhausted by their conflict, she lay down in the bed beside him.

"The bastard," She thought. "He could always defuse a crisis with his humor."

Hours passed while she considered all her options. Finally, she decided what she had to do before she could live with the situation. As she drifted off to sleep, her decision made her smile.

CHAPTER TWELVE

Samantha awakened suddenly. She rolled over and stared at the bright red numerals of her bedside clock. It read five after five in the morning. She listened intently for any unusual sounds. She heard nothing except the steady breathing emanating from Dave, whose prone body lay beside her.

"Nothing ever fazes him." Samantha mused. "Yesterday, he came home to a wronged woman and I verbally emasculated him. And, what was his reaction to my tirade? He simply crawled into our bed and quickly fell fast asleep.

I wonder; is he awake? I'm sure he isn't. But, I'll lie here for a few minutes just to make certain."

Minutes passed. His breathing remained steady. She moved one leg off the bed and then carefully peeled back the covers. When both feet were on the floor, she rose and silently made her way to the bathroom. Once through with her morning's routine, she put on tight shorts and a loose blouse. Both, of which, revealed what she wanted Desmond to know she possessed.

Slowly, she descended the stairs, walked into the kitchen, picked up her cell phone, and texted; "Are you there?"

Samantha smiled as she read the response; "We're up. Can you drive to my place this morning?"

"Of course; any particular reason you want me to drive?" Samantha responded.

"Yes; I have a gift for you." He teased.

"How nice and what did I do to earn a gift?" Samantha smiled, as she texted her response. Then she murmured out loud; "He probably has something in mind that I might be able to do in the near future. I wonder what that might be." She smiled, in mock innocence.

She smiled again as she read his response; "Just for you being you; is your reward. Anyway, I'll see you shortly."

Samantha replied with a succinct; "Okay; see you in a bit. I'm gone."

After folding her cell phone, she slipped out the front door, got into her car, and quietly drove off. Five minutes later, she pulled into Desmond's driveway. Immediately, he was along side her car, opening the door for her. She clasped his extended hand as she rose from her car seat. Desmond backed away, reluctantly, to allow her standing room and then commented.

"Sam, without make up and with your hair down; you're the most beautiful women on the planet." He whispered, in a voice made husky by his anticipation of delights that might be forthcoming.

What Desmond said was exactly the kind of thing she had hoped to hear. But, now that he had said it, she was uncertain how to respond. She didn't want to discourage his attention. But, she didn't want him to think she would be easy. She decided to parry his compliment with an ambiguous smile.

Desmond suspected Samantha's reaction might mean that their relationship could only be platonic. However, the way she tilted her head towards him, allayed his fears and suggested his patience might eventually be rewarded.

Somewhat embarrassed, Desmond confessed that he had inadvertently lowered the garage door.

"Bear with me. I'll be right back." Desmond said, as he disappeared around the corner of the house on his way to the front door.

As she waited at the closed garage door, she realized she was annoyed with her rejection of the possibility of a casual encounter with someone like Desmond. But, her contempt for Dave's promiscuous behavior had destroyed any desire to emulate it. It was one thing to dream about casual sex. It was quite another to run the risks associated with it. But, then she began to ponder what the risks to her marriage might really be.

"What would Dave say if I left the house to go jogging in a see-through blouse and came back with the buttons of my shorts undone? Certainly Dave would look the other way. I suspect, in a way, he would be relieved; for then he would have someone with whom he could share shame.

But, it's really not the Dave types that enslave women. It's the ones that put women on pedestals and refuse to let them be human. I just wonder. Is a Merry Queen comfortable sitting on her throne?"

Samantha was beginning to realize that if she were going to be truly happy, she would have to resolve the conflicts between what she wanted to do and what society insisted she do. She knew that the inhibitions in the psyche of her gender had been put there by thousands of years of exposure to societies designed by males to promote male interests. She actually marveled how male power had created a subservient role for women in all societies throughout history by creating religions dominated by male gods. To be truly free, she was going to have to live with some guilt until she could discard the constraints that made her feel comfortable only in the kitchen. It was socially tolerated for Dave to carouse. But for Samantha to cavort, she would have to be comfortable with conduct less virtuous than what she now considered acceptable.

She envied Frances Van Cleve's freedom. Although she didn't admire Frances' conduct, it no longer disgusted her. She realized that the increasing awareness of how women were treated in Muslim societies had revealed similar, but more subtle abuses, in her own society. She knew God existed. But like other honest people, she had no real understanding of His ways. He had given her a body that she felt belonged entirely to her. She was beginning to realize, if she honored its instincts, she would experience joy. If she allowed others to convince her to ignore those instincts, she would suffer.

In the short time it had taken Desmond to reach the inside of the garage, she had made a profound decision. She would suffer Dave's perfidy. But, she would carefully examine the wisdom of suppressing her own yearnings.

Suddenly, the garage door started moving. When it was partially open, a bent over Desmond emerged from under the rising door.

"Now Samantha, if you will follow me, I'll take you to what I've made for you." He said, as he straightened up and took her hand.

"Okay Desmond, I'm with you."

Samantha followed him into the dark garage staying close behind him to avoid contact with all kinds of tools and machines. Once through the garage, he opened the back door to the house and they entered a dimly lit laundry room. After he closed the door behind them, he tapped Samantha on the shoulder and when she turned to face him, he asked if Dave had returned from his trip.

A moment passed while Samantha considered whether to tell Desmond the truth or just tell him a white lie. She decided that a white lie would be the easiest response.

"The trip was fine. But, I could tell that things in England didn't go particularly well." Then, she added almost maliciously, "We had a couple issues we had to resolve. But then, we settled down and enjoyed a quiet evening."

Samantha thought to herself. "I wonder why I added that nonsense, I just said. I suspect it's because I'm proud of the way I verbally kicked Dave's philandering ass. I really wanted to tell Desmond the truth. But, I don't like to burden other people with my personal problems."

Finished musing, she turned to Desmond and asked.

"Where's the surprise? You do have one, don't you?" She asked in mock distrust.

"Oh yes, I certainly do. Just stay close to me and you'll be pleased." Desmond insisted, with a voice whose lack of authority was compromised by the conflict between what he wanted to say and what he thought he should say.

They moved through the darkened house and then descended to the lower level. At the bottom of the stairs he took her hand and led her to a bedroom door. She hesitated until he reached into the room and switched on a light revealing an exquisite hand carved easel.

"It's beautiful!" She gasped, as she pressed her fingers against her lips.

"How could you have made such an elegant thing in the short time I've known you?" She exclaimed, as she stroked its rounded frame.

"It's just absolutely beautiful!" She repeated.

"How can I possibly show my appreciation?" She queried, as she threw her arms around Desmond's neck and pulled his chest against her breasts.

"There may be a charge, like a fervent kiss." He whispered into her ear as he flicked a wall switch to plunge the room into total darkness. His arms still around her he tumbled them down onto the bed. Lying on top of her he forced his knee between her legs and pressed his swollen groin against her abdomen. She opened her mouth to protest, but before she could he forced his tongue between her lips and into her open mouth. Suddenly aroused she fiercely returned his kiss. Deftly he drew her blouse down around her waist and gently freed her soft breasts. She moaned as he fondled one erect nipple and then the other.

Impatiently he pulled and tugged at her shorts. She reached down and released a reluctant button. Loosened, he pulled them over her hips and down around her knees. Suddenly he stood up. Samantha lay there, aching for his attention as she listened to the quiet hum of a descending zipper and the soft sound of his clothing hitting the floor. Naked he bent over her and stripped off her disheveled clothes and then laid down between her widely spread legs. Gently he entered her. Frantic, Samantha wrapped her legs around his back and arched her hips to accommodate the growing insistence of his powerful thrusts. Suddenly it was over and they lay quietly together, exhausted.

Moments passed then Desmond whispered. "Do you know that it's almost 8, Sam?"

"Are you serious?! I've got to fly. Let me use your bathroom. My clothes are a mess and I expect my hair is too." Samantha screamed, as she picked up her clothes off the floor and disappeared into the bathroom.

Struggling to smooth out the wrinkles in her shorts and her blouse, she caught a glimpse of herself in the mirror.

"Damn, I look like I've been doing a Comanche buck. If Dave sees me in these shorts and this blouse, he'll have a field day sneering at my explanation, after the thumping I gave him yesterday. I've got to get back there before the bastard wakes up. I don't have a comb. How am I going to make this rat's nest look presentable? Oh hell, what can I do with it?" Samantha cried out as she patted down her hair with water.

Finally realizing she could do no more to improve her appearance, she rushed out of the bathroom and up the stairs. As she brushed by Desmond, she lightly landed a kiss of endearment on his cheek.

"I'll text you as soon as I get the opportunity." She called out from the top of the stairs and then added. "When do I get my gift?" She asked, but disappeared through the open front door before Desmond could answer her question.

On her way home, she considered various explanations she might concoct to explain her appearance. She couldn't think of any explanation that Dave might buy. She was desperate and in an absolute panic when she turned onto her street and Dave's Mini Cooper wasn't in the driveway. Overwhelmed with relief, she parked her car in the driveway and bolted into the house. As she expected, Dave had left a note. He would be back in an hour.

She breathed a sigh of relief. She knew she had been fortunate. She also knew if there was a next time, she might not be so lucky, and that scared her very much. But, what really terrified her was the thought that there might not be a next time.

CHAPTER THIRTEEN

An impeccably dressed Samantha sat by the window in the front room of her home. Every few minutes she glanced out at their driveway hoping to see Dave's car appear. When she wasn't looking out the window, she closed her eyes and a smile formed on her attractive face as she recalled her early morning experience with Desmond. She felt wonderful. She had no feelings of guilt, even though, in the back of her mind, she suspected her conduct and her choice of attire had inappropriately encouraged Desmond. If they had, she admitted to herself, she was not sorry. But, her feelings towards Dave were another thing. They had gone from contempt to resignation. She actually admired the way he used his intellect to go after anything his teen age passions craved.

She had spent the hour, since she had returned from Desmond's, grooming herself in preparation for a late morning meeting at the Police Department with Molly and a F.B.I. agent. The meeting had been planned to discuss all the issues with the F.B.I. agent and to make Dave aware that his clandestine activities were now out in the open. The night before, Samantha had been so intent on verbally abusing Dave, she had forgotten to tell him about the meeting. She expected Dave's return shortly and when he arrived she was going to fill him in on the need for the meeting. She suspected he might prove difficult. If he did, Samantha was mulling over, in her mind, what she might say to convince him that it was in his best interest to attend the meeting.

Suddenly, Dave's car pulled into the driveway. A moment passed and he walked into the house. He looked askance at Samantha and when he saw the outfit she had on, he suspected something out of the ordinary was planned. He sat down opposite her and waited patiently for his wife to drop the hammer. He suspected that she had been in contact with a divorce lawyer and that she was about to insist he attend some meeting to discuss what she was going to demand in a divorce action. However, he was puzzled by the change in her demeanor from the night before. She appeared relaxed, warm, and not the least bit vindictive. At her invitation, he sat down in the chair she indicated. At first, she just stared at him as though reluctant to broach a difficult subject. Dave stared back and thought to himself;

"She's beautiful. Maybe I've been forgiven. Maybe she feels sorry for having damn near crucified me. Maybe she wants makeup sex. You're crazy; that goddamn thing between your legs is doing your thinking again. You've got to get him under control."

"Dave," Samantha interrupted his pondering by softly saying his name. "The day you left for London I was attacked, while jogging in the woods. The man was prevented from raping me by the intercession of another jogger. I was not hurt. But my assailant, after he had been subdued, accused me of attempting to hire him to murder you.

After the police got involved, they concluded that someone might have hired the man who attacked me. They suspected it might have been you. So they requested that I not tell you about the attack until they had cleared you as a suspect. Subsequently, they cleared you. But, during their investigation, other issues surfaced that involved you. They would now like us to come down to the police station and discuss the whole situation. The tentative meeting is scheduled for 11 am. Do you have any problem attending the meeting with me?"

"Hold it, hold it Sam; what do you mean you were attacked in the woods? Why didn't you tell me? That's mind boggling." Dave blurted out. But, before he could continue, Samantha interrupted him.

"Look Dave, I was pretty shook up, especially when my assailant counter charged me with trying to hire him to murder you. The police, who were very considerate, said it was a 'he said- you said' case and obtaining a conviction in court might be difficult."

"That doesn't make sense. Why couldn't the guy who rescued you testify?"

"I heard Desmond running through the brush towards me, and just before he arrived, I pushed Coirpeach as hard as I could. He fell backwards onto his knees, just as Desmond entered the clearing. All Desmond saw was Coirpeach on his knees trying to protect himself from my blows."

"Wait a second. Who's Desmond and who the hell is Coirpeach?"

Samantha explained who they were and what they had done during the episode that took place in the woods. When she finished, Dave reluctantly agreed to attend the meeting. Dave, being Dave, suspected that if he cooperated, it might gain the favor he now coveted with Samantha.

At eleven o'clock, Molly Malone ushered Dave and Samantha into a small conference room in the police station where Molly introduced them to FBI agent Jack Welch.

After fitting introductions, Molly began the meeting by detailing her hypothesis.

"Our investigation, to date, has led us to believe that Wilber Coirpeach was hired by someone to attack Samantha and we suspect that that someone might be Intimidator Inc.

We are aware that you, Mr. O'Connor, sold worthless mortgage-backed securities to the city of Chekhov and that the city fathers of Chekhov hired Intimidator Inc. to try and recoup their losses.

We know that you were having an affair with Frances Van Cleve and one Elizabeth Foster in the U.K. and that Intimidator Inc. used that information to extort money from you.

Now, your personal affairs are not our concern, unless you know something that we can use to determine who hired Wilber Coirpeach to criminally attack your wife. If you do, please tell us now."

When Molly finished speaking, everyone turned and stared at Dave, who averted everyone's eyes by staring out the window. After a long pause, Dave looked at Samantha and began to speak.

"I know that I probably should consult an attorney before I open my mouth. But, I certainly had nothing to do with the attack on my wife, whom I truly love. Samantha told me about it only just this morning and I was appalled. One thing I can say for certain; Intimidator Inc. is a class operation. There's no way they would ever be involved in something as heinous as arranging an attack on an innocent woman. They didn't extort money from me. They simply asked me to make a donation to a city that I materially helped bankrupt. I might add though, that what I did was not illegal. It was a legitimate business deal that went wrong."

"Do you have any idea who might have been behind the attack on your wife?" Molly asked again, while ignoring his plea for understanding.

"I have no idea, what so ever, absolutely none." Dave replied forcefully.

"Mr. O'Connor, would you briefly describe to us what your responsibilities are as a vice president of Honrado Bank?" A laid back Jack Welch asked.

Dave turned towards him but did not immediately respond to his request. There was something about agent Welch that made Dave think very carefully about what he was going to say to him before saying it. Agent Welch had an aura about him that conveyed the message that it would be unwise to tell Agent Welch anything but the gospel truth.

"As you probably know, Agent Welch, Honrado is an investment bank. My main function at the bank; is to create mortgaged backed securities that consist of diversely rated home mortgages. Most of the securities include subprime mortgages that have been combined with higher quality mortgages to create a triple 'A' rated product. As an agent of the bank, I sell that product to investors. The bank earns substantial fees for this function and when the products are sold to investors, the bank's liability usually ends. However, the bank continues to earn management fees as long as the mortgage owners continue to make their monthly payments."

"It's my understanding that a subprime mortgage is one granted to someone who is a border line qualifier. Is that right Mr. O'Connor?" Agent Welch inquired and then asked.

"Why would any bank loan money to someone who was unlikely to pay it back?"

"Well, if the price of houses had continued to climb, the likelihood of subprime mortgages being honored would have been reasonably good. However, that all changed when the value of houses declined dramatically."

"And what caused the sudden decline, Mr. O'Connor?" Agent Welch asked.

"The FED raised the interest rate and when that happened abruptly, millions of people could not make their mortgage payments."

"Now Mr. O'Connor, when the bank sells a mortgage-backed security, it's true that the bank re-coups their capital, isn't? Well if that's the case, it would appear to me a need would develop for more and more mortgage seekers. Wouldn't that need tend to lower mortgage qualification requirements?"

"And that's exactly what happened, Agent Welch. As I said, the originating and packaging of loans earn banks substantial fees and make loan volume far more important than loan quality."

"Well Mr. O'Connor, I don't see any role in this whole process, for a fiduciary."

"I understand why you don't, Agent Welch, because there isn't any." Dave shot back and then added; "When things began to slow down, investors began to insist on a "buy back" provision. Then when home prices collapsed, some loan originators didn't have the cash to buy back the mortgages and had to go into bankruptcy. That's what happened to Bear Steers and others."

"How did this whole mess get started?" Agent Welch asked.

"Essentially, it was a regulatory failure. If all your competitors are making money legally by a procedure blessed by the government, a bank has to do as everybody else does, or its board of directors will fire the CEO."

"I assume that people who found their investment worthless were not happy and very angry with the person that sold them the mortgage-backed securities."

"Well," Dave replied, "That certainly was true of the city fathers of Chekhov."

"Thank you Mr. O'Connor for your primer on the financial disaster we've just gone through. Or, maybe I should say, are going through. But now, let's get back to the reason why we're all here. It seems to me that Intimidator Inc. is not involved with the attack on you, Mrs. O'Connor. What do you think, Molly?"

"Please excuse me for interrupting, Ms. Malone, but before you respond to Agent Welch's question, I would like to comment further on the country's financial situation."

"Certainly, Mr. O'Connor, please do." Molly agreed.

"Thank you, Ms. Malone. IBGUBG is an acronym widely used to promote questionable dealings between various financial companies in the U.S. and in Europe. Defined, it means; 'I'll be gone and you'll be gone.' It's used by highly paid executives and it simply means that if a pending deal results in a catastrophic lost and they get fired, they'll still walk away with a fistful of cash. The root cause of our recent financial crisis, and it will be the root cause of future financial crises, is the exorbitant salaries and in what coin they are paid. By coin, I mean stock options. Executives at banks and other financial companies take great risks to boost their company's stock price because it directly affects their income. What can Government regulations do to control this type of conduct? Very little, because elected members of both political parties depend on contributions from these companies to stay in office."

"What can be done, Mr O'Connor, to prevent the next crises?" Agent Welch asked.

"In my opinion, nothing short of a revolution will solve the problem."

"Well, thank you Mr.O'Connor. But, what has this mess in the financial companies got to do with the issues we're discussing here?" Agent Welch asked again.

"Well, a lot of us in the business would like to see the government create sensible regulations that would stop the crazy gambling that is now prevalent. So, anytime we come in contact with a representative of a Federal agency, we unload on him hoping he might be able to do something our elected representatives refuse to do. We know you can't do anything to rectify the situation, but it makes us feel better complaining to you."

When Dave finished answering Agent Welch's question, he turned to Molly and apologized for interrupting the procedure and asked her to voice any concerns she might be harboring.

"The only thing bothering me is the call from London that came in on Coirpeach's cell phone. Ms Selkirk thought that the man she let use her phone might have had a slight accent- possibly Russian. I'm not comfortable dismissing the implications of that phone call. Is there anyone you know in the U.K. who might have orchestrated the attack on your wife, Mr. O'Connor?"

"Ms. Malone, I've only known about the attacked on Sam for a couple of hours. Maybe after I've had time to think about it, I might come up with something. But at the moment, I don't have a clue."

"I certainly hope you can, Mr. O'Connor, because if you can't, Wilber Coirpeach might very well walk."

After Dave reluctantly accepted that Wilber Coirpeach would probably go free, he shook hands with Molly and Agent Welch. Then he turned to Samantha, took her arm, and the two of them walked out of the police station together.

After Samantha and Dave had gone, Agent Welch turned to Molly and said;

"Dave may not be perfect. But, he does have some redeeming qualities. He certainly knows his job. I think if we're patient, Molly, he may come up with something for you to go on. It may be too early to conclude, but at the moment, it doesn't look like there's a role here for the FBI. If things change, let me know.

"Well thanks for coming by anyway, Jack. I'm sorry I got you involved in this thing. But, at one time, it looked like Intimidator Inc. was the culprit. However now, I certainly agree, it doesn't look that way anymore. I do expect, though, the phone call is going to bother me for a long time, unless Mr. O'Connor comes up with something."

"I agree, Molly. It certainly is a loose end. Whoever's behind the attack appears to be crafty enough to have placed the call with the intent of leading us astray. My intuition leads me to believe it's someone here in the U.S.A. The way the O'Connor's credit card was used to cast suspicion on Mr. O'Connor, suggests whoever it is has lots of resources at their disposal. Maybe Mr. O'Connor will come up with some ideas when he has had time to think about it.

As far as Intimidator Inc. is concerned, you did the right thing, Molly. Had they been involved, it would have been our baby. Anyway, I've got to run. I'm due in court this afternoon. You have a good day and if you do get to the bottom of this mystery, please give me a call."

When agent Welch finished speaking, he and Molly shook hands and parted.

CHAPTER FOURTEEN

As Samantha and Dave drove home from their meeting with Agent Welch and Molly, Dave turned to Samantha and commented;

"Sam, you didn't say much in the meeting. What do you think?"

"You sure said plenty. Do you own stock in Intimidator Inc.?" Samantha asked, sarcastically.

"I had to give those people four hundred thousands bucks. They're a legitimate charity case. I'm going to claim them as tax deduction."

"You're not serious?" Samantha cried out and then moaned. "You're incredible!"

"What do you mean? I didn't do anything legally culpable. If you've got a bitch, it's with the do-nothing politicians. They have the responsibility to make the rules. I just go along with what they say is legal."

"Don't you have any decency at all?" Samantha gasped.

"My guide is the Good Book." Dave claimed, in a taunting, sanctimonious, tone.

"What do you know, Dave, about the Good Book?"

"Well, doesn't it say; 'Seest thou a man diligent in his business? He shall be honored by kings. Mean men shall not scorn him.'?"

"I assume your 'mean men' are bank regulators?" Samantha countered, in a taunting tone of her own, and then added;

"It also says; 'Hell hath no fury like a woman scorned.' And you're going to find out how true that statement is!"

Dave said nothing. But he thought to himself; doesn't look good for make up sex. Damn, but then there's always Frances.

After a period of silence, Dave announced as they approached their house, that he was going to drop her off and continue on to his office. After Dave stopped the car in their driveway, Samantha turned and asked him, as she prepared to leave the vehicle, when he would be home.

"It's hard to say. I could be late. I'll call you when I can be more definite."

Samantha just stared at him, for a long moment, and then got out of the car.

"She's a bitch." He said out loud after Samantha had violently slammed the car door shut.

While driving to his office, Dave began to wonder who had hired Wilber Coirpeach to attack Samantha. He couldn't think of one person who would do such a thing to Samantha. He had his enemies, he knew. But, he couldn't imagine any one of them hating him so much that they would risk going to jail. As he drove into the company parking complex, he concluded that Coirpeach had hit on the wrong women. It had all been a mistake. Satisfied with his conclusion, he put the whole incident out his mind as he walked into his office.

"Dave! What a pleasant surprise." His smiling assistant, Ms. Carolyn, gushed as she rose to greet him.

"No need to fuss. Here it is." Dave said, in mock sincerity, as he handed her a small box.

"Dave, you shouldn't have. You know the company policy about giving gifts." Ms. Carolyn cautioned, with a broad smile which turned mischievous, as she opened her gift.

"Thank you Mr. O'Connor; they're beautiful." She exclaimed, as she resisted the urge to immediately replace the modest ear rings she was wearing, with them.

"They must have cost you a fortune."

"No matter what they cost, Kathy, it was insignificant when compared to the contribution you make around here."

Dave had great respect for his assistant. She was extremely attractive. But more importantly, she was extremely competent. He often worried about the possibility of her resigning. In fact, he was terrified by that thought. He knew she understood a lot more about the banking business then he did.

"Well Cathy; it's great to be back. What's the most pressing issue I have to address?" Dave asked.

"It's a strange one. Ron Filbert has called me every day this week, reminding me that he has something extremely important that he has to discuss with you and it has to be done as soon as you arrive back. Do you want me to call and tell him you're in the office now?"

"Yes; and tell him I'll see him as soon as he's available. While I'm waiting for Ron, I'll go through my mail. Is it in the in-box?" Dave asked, as he entered his office.

"Yes, it's all there." Kathy replied, as she dialed Ron's phone number. When he answered, she simply said; "He's here and will see you as soon as you can get here." After cradling the phone, she went to the door of Dave's office and said; "He's on his way."

Five minutes later, a grim looking Ron Filbert stood before her desk; "Can I go in?" Ron asked. Kathy answered positively by waving her hand, palm up, towards the door of Dave's office.

Ron Filbert was a close personal friend of Dave's. Both were champion bridge players who had won national tournaments playing together as partners. He reported directly to Charles Van Cleve, who considered him to be the best quantitative analyst in the financial world. Ron had to be on-board on any financial project before Charlie would sign off on it.

Once inside Dave's office, Ron closed the door behind him, pulled up a chair to the side of Dave's desk and sat down in it. He took out a small pad from his suit pocket. Placed it on Dave's desk, and wrote; "Where can we talk?"

Dave reached into his desk and brought out a piece of paper and scribbled on it; "across the street at the restaurant in a half an hour."

Ron read Dave's note, nodded affirmatively, pushed back the chair as he stood up, and walked out of Dave's office.

Kathy looked up at Ron. Neither spoke as he rushed by her. After he had gone, Kathy got up from her desk and walked into Dave's office.

"Ron seemed upset. Is there anything I can do?" She asked.

"Thanks Kathy." Dave whispered, and continued in barely audible voice. "But, I really don't know what the problem is yet. We're going to meet across the street at the restaurant in a half an hour. If I can tell you, I'll let you know when I get back."

A half hour later, Dave walked into the restaurant and looked around to see Ron, sitting in a booth, at the back of the almost empty restaurant. Dave moved quickly to Ron's table and as he sat down, Dave said:

"I know there must be a crisis, Ron. But, by the way you look, I'm not sure I want to know the details." Dave quipped and then added; "What the hell is it?"

"Charlie accessed your personal account." Ron whispered.

"How do you know that?" A suddenly very alert, Dave asked.

"He told me the day after you left for London. He also told me, that he knew, you had done Frances, on numerous occasions, and that you were going to soon find out how it feels when someone does your wife. If he knew I was telling you this, I would be out of a job today."

"I wouldn't worry about that, Ron." A grim faced Dave advised. "He's using you as a messenger. He knows damn well that you and I are buddies and that you would relay his message. The old bastard, I didn't think he still had the sauce in his groin to let a little thing like someone banging his trophy wife, bother him. He could have been a little bit more considerate of Sam, though. I don't think a roll in the weeds with a hired scumbag would have been something she would have relished. But, then you never know; women are strange."

"You shock me Dave. I just can't understand you're cavalier attitude. If I were involved in anything like this, I couldn't handle it. Hell, I can see wheels turning in your head. I know what you're thinking; how can I profit from this whole mess? You're cool Dave, very cool. What are you going to do?"

"You know what I'm going to do. I've already started; I'm going to think. You've played enough bridge with me to know that I never complain about the cards dealt me; I just play them as well as I can. This is an opportunity for us to get perpetual job security. Charlie's a good guy. He just went off the deep end. For my forgiveness, I'm sure he'll want to pay me well." Dave paused and looked up at the ceiling and then continued.

"I don't think there's any need for us to share what we know with Sam." He paused again, and then smiled as he added; "She might not understand. If she reacted unwisely, you and I might end up broke and Charlie might end up in the slammer. Now, we do not want that to happen. Life is good when you have a clear conscience and lots of money."

"If you're ready, Ron, we can now saunter back to the office, together."

CHAPTER FIFTEEN

As soon as Dave arrived back from his meeting with Ron, he had Kathy call Charlie's secretary and set up a late afternoon meeting. Alone in his office, he pondered how he would start the meeting. He wasn't sure whether to be submissive or aggressive. He finally decided that since Charlie was still the boss, he should at least initially be both humble and subtle. Several hours later after considering how he would respond to any eventuality, a confident Dave entered Charlie's office after gently knocking on its partially open door.

Charlie was alone in the office. He was standing by a window looking out at the East River. He turned slowly and politely motioned Dave towards a plush leather chair that had been pulled up to the front of his large desk. Both men sat down cautiously. Charlie initiated the conversation. He spoke very slowly, like a man whose age had begun to weigh on him.

"By now, Dave, I assume you've talked to Ron Filbert. Is that correct?" Charlie asked quietly.

"Well Charlie, let me say this. I don't want to involve anyone else in our conflict. However, I do know you arranged to have Wilber Coirpeach assault my wife. I understand your motive. But that doesn't mean I condone your action. However, I do accept some responsibility for driving you to the despair you must have experienced when you discovered a liaison existed between your wife and me. Certainly your loss of self esteem had to be a major factor that drove you to the felonious act of commissioning someone to commit such a serious crime."

Dave's use of the word "felonious" caused Charlie's complexion to redden. When he meekly accepted Dave's characterization of his crime, Dave knew that Charlie had come to his senses and that Charlie now realized he might have to face the consequences of having committed a felony. The thought terrified him. Dave, recognizing Charlie's growing panic was rendering him defenseless, went on to stress that Dave's own offense was not illegal. Dave paused to give Charlie time to consider what might happen if he had to defend himself in a court of law. Satisfied that Charlie's guilt and fear had reduced his complaints of Dave's indiscretion to a whimper; Dave verbally continued to subtly emasculate a defenseless Charlie.

"It's true, Charlie, that Frances and I have had consensual sex that was mutually initiated. I have the highest respect for Frances. I do not condemn her; for I don't know the nature of the force that drives her behavior. Only God knows what the demons in her soul, crave. Certainly, she offended her marriage vows. But, man created the institution of marriage. Like all things created by man; it has its imperfections. I admire Frances' courage. I do not agree with our society's condemnation of women who have extramarital affairs while men's indiscretions are dismissed as benign. For one reason or another she has a need for affection. You, perhaps, know the root cause of that. What she needs now is your understanding and forgiveness. I'm beseeching you to embrace and forgive her. As for my own conduct which initiated this whole ugly affair, I'm truly sorry."

When Dave finished speaking, Charlie rose slowly from his chair and awkwardly walked over to the window. Once there he again stared out at the East river. After what seemed a long time, he absent-mindedly closed the blinds on the window. Returning to his desk, he sank into his chair- a diminished and deflated man. A moment passed. Charlie raised himself to an erect sitting position, made eye contact with Dave, and began to plead for Dave's forgiveness in a low steady voice.

"Dave, if you will permit me, before I respond to what you've said, I would like to quote from the Bible."

Dave merely nodded his head in approval and Charlie began. "'For now we see through a glass, darkly; but then face to face: now I know in part; but then shall I know even as also I am known.' Saint Paul's message is simply that no human being can ever be certain how they will react to any event or injury because they can never really see themselves as they really are. I was appalled, and remain so, by my maniacal need to avenge the injury that you inflicted upon my self esteem by illicitly consorting with Frances. Had I realized the extent of my penchant to react violently, when offended, I could have dealt more effectively with the issue by first conquering myself. Now that I have accomplished that, I'm asking you to understand and forgive me for plotting to subject you to a terrible vengeance.

However Dave, it still remains that we have greatly offended one another. My misdeed is the more heinous in that I sought to subject an innocent woman to an unspeakable ordeal. I thank God, every waking moment, that the experience I had plan for Samantha, to endure, did not take place. Please accept my heartfelt apology."

Dave thought to himself; that's right Charlie. You lost your head. Now you've lost your wife's respect and your power over me. You're lucky though. I'll forgive you now that you've made me an unofficial partner of your bank.

"Charlie, you've been like a father to me, and I've rewarded you by stealing the affection of your wife and driving you to a desperation that could have ruined both our lives. I'm an ingrate and I do not deserve to have you as a friend. I've done you a great disservice and it's with a humble heart that I beseech you to put this matter behind us and renew our friendship."

"Thank you Dave." Then after a long pause, Charlie added. "As of this moment let us consider the issue resolved and give thanks to the Lord for what he has revealed to us about ourselves."

"Thank you for giving our friendship another chance, Charlie." Dave exclaimed in a contrite manner he had mastered by having had to deliver it many times during his life.

They shook hands and while doing so they looked intently into one another's eyes. Charlie knew that Dave had won the struggle. He was looking into Dave's eyes to see if he was going to be merciful. Dave was staring back at Charlie telling him that he would not abuse the new power he now possessed. When they ended their handshake, Charlie sighed, for he knew a dangerous situation had been resolved by his willingness to put down the 'dark glass' and truly look at himself 'face to face'.

On his way back to his office, Dave stopped by Ron's office. Ron looked up from his desk to see a smiling Dave; standing in his office doorway thrusting a thumb up fist towards him. Dave said nothing. He turned and walked away leaving a speechless Ron, with a slight smile on his face, shaking his head in disbelief.

On reaching his office, Dave slouched into the chair behind his desk and let out a sigh of relieve. The crisis had passed. After a respite, he began to verbally muse about his other pressing problem.

"What the hell am I going to do about Frances? She's going to want to be serviced. I wonder if the old man has broached the subject with her. Probably not; he's probably going to look the other way. Maybe he wouldn't mind if I rang her bell every once in awhile. Frances is kind of a nice problem. It will be fun working with her to find a solution.

Samantha, God I don't know what to do with her. I wonder if there's anything to the stories I hear about aphrodisiacs. I may as well forget that; if they existed, they wouldn't work on her anyway. One thing is for sure. I can't tell her the truth. If I did, that cute little nut cracker, Molly, would eventually be all over poor Charlie. He's got to be protected. He feels so guilty now that all Ms. Malone would have to do is bark and he would confess to murdering Lucy Borden's parents. Maybe I should have spent more time easing his feelings of guilt. But it's a tough call; ease too much and you encourage your adversary to see your offense as being flawed. I really don't like to think about the police hassling Charlie. I'm glad agent Welch is no longer involved in the investigation. Had he talked to Charlie, it would have been all over in five minutes. I've got to keep Charlie under wraps for at least six months. God, it makes me shiver to think of what could happen if he crumbles. It's getting late. I best call the dreaded one and let her know I'm on my way home."

After Dave talked to Samantha, he walked to his car and as he drove home, he continued to mull over various options. He could tell Samantha the truth. But, he knew that would be courting disaster. He had to convince her that Coirpeach had simply hit on the wrong women. He knew she wouldn't buy it immediately. But, he felt he could convince her eventually, given enough time, that it was in her best interest to believe the whole thing was a case of mistaken identity. He had to drive a wedge between Samantha and Molly Malone. He knew that Samantha and Ms. Malone were buddies. He also knew that it was only a matter of time before Ms. Malone began to see Charlie as a potential suspect. If that happened, he would have to come clean with Samantha and convince her to save Charlie's hide by refusing to testify against Coirpeach. Dave felt that he might be able to sell the idea, to Samantha, that his affair with Frances had temporarily destroyed Charlie's good sense and that he, Dave himself, was ultimately responsible for Charlie's reprehensible action. Dave suspected it would be an easy sell because he knew he would be selling the truth. Accepting his guilt and his readiness to pay some price for his culpability made him feel good. He thought to himself; no wonder the "do-gooders" of this world like to do good works.

He began to verbalize his thoughts. "That will appeal to Sam. She's really never going to be happy until she sees me hung up like a wild eyed stag on her studio wall. Damn it; women are indispensable. They're like beautiful roses. But, if you handle them carelessly, they sure can make you bleed.

I wonder how Charlie found Coirpeach? He couldn't have dealt with him directly. It had to be that guy who's in charge of security. He's an ex-cop. He would know people like Coirpeach. A wise choice; he owes Charlie big time. His son had some kind of weird illness and Charlie paid for all of the kid's medical bills. It's very unlikely that deal will ever unravel.

As far as Charlie accommodating me, that was a good business move. He gets to stay out of jail and he retains his best crisis manager. Both of us know the mortgage monster is going to get bigger and a lot uglier before it goes away. Hell, I suspect a lot of banks packaged and sold mortgages that they never even bothered to scrutinize. It's going to be a field day for the lawyers. It annoys the hell out me just thinking about how much time we're going to have to spend in court defending ourselves from that redundant gang of parasites. They're going to feast on us. I suppose we should have thought about that before we put our hands in the cookie jar.

It's humorous how generous we can be to those who offend us, if we need them. Love thine enemy is a great hedge. Anyone who has to turn a cheek to an enemy, that he needs, can do so with honor. However, if an enemy is unimportant to you and he sticks a sharp stick into your eye, it's perfectly okay for you to respond in kind.

We're such a slick species. I feel so at ease belonging to it. Despite the denial of the righteous; if the need arises, we'll all make ourselves comfortable by using guile to extricate ourselves from a desperate situation. Who in their heart of hearts can condemn the felon who steals to feed his innocent children? Who will be able to condemn the conduct of the American middle class when they guillotine us for growing wealthy by selling their jobs to the Chinese? The meek will inherit the earth. But, if they don't have jobs, they may put six feet of their earth over our headless bodies.

But enough now; I'll leave worrying about highly improbable catastrophes to the talking heads on T.V. Potentially, I could have an unpleasant situation on my hands if I can't get sanctimonious

Samantha to forgive my wayward ways, and let me enjoy her lovely endowments. It would be humiliating to have to follow her around panting like a satyr, craving to fondle what she has stuffed into a tight pair of slacks and a revealing blouse. I can covet all I want. But only patience and guile will annul the wrath of a wronged woman. I know celibacy is to be my punishment. I probably can endure the agony. But if it threatens to overwhelm me, there's always friendly Frances. What am I saying? I just got out of that jam and I'm already thinking of enjoying her favors again. I'm a slow learner." Dave concluded, as he parked his car in the driveway.

"We're here; might as well go in and start the sentence." He mumbled as he exited the car and walked towards the front door of his house; where a radiant Samantha stood holding it ajar for him.

Struck by how attractive she appeared, Dave mumbled to himself. "It's beginning. She looks like Helen of Troy. I won't be able to touch her. But it sure will be pleasant looking at her. Damn, I wish I had a hat that I could carry in my hand, as I approach her"

"Hi Sam; you look beautiful." Dave gasped, cheerfully.

"Thank you, Dave." Samantha hissed and then continued in the same tone. "It's a little late for your clever tongue to try and undo the consequences of what your other thoughtless appendage has done."

Dave said nothing as he slipped passed her and entered the house. Samantha closed the door behind him. Without saying another word, she went directly to the kitchen leaving him standing in the middle of their living room clutching his imaginary hat. Left with nothing to say or do, Dave climbed the stairs to the second floor. As he approached their bedroom, he glanced into Samantha's well lit studio and was stunned to see the portrait of himself as an old man.

"God, I think that's me. Well, I hope she put most of her venom into it. If she didn't, that's what I'm going to look like when she finishes punishing me." Dave exclaimed as he walked past Samantha's studio and into their bedroom.

"Well no matter. I know what will restore me and I think I'll just slide into bed and think about it until the warden summons me to an unsavory snack."

That said, Dave lay down on the bed and was soon fast asleep, with a smile on his face.